MOCHIMA

Copyright © 2025 Rick Cameron

This is a work of fiction. Names, characters, and incidents are either the product of the author's imagination or are used fictitiously. Any resemblance to actual persons, living or dead, business, companies, events or locales is entirely coincidental. Most of the locations herein are also fictional or used fictitiously. However, the author takes great pains to depict the locations and descriptions of these islands and locales throughout these islands and the northern coast of South America to the best of his ability.

Printed in the United States of America.

ISBN: 978-1-63385-552-6
Library of Congress Control Number: 2025913720

Published by
Word Association Publishers
205 Fifth Avenue
Tarentum, Pennsylvania 15084

www.wordassociation.com
1.800.827.7903

MOCHIMA

A Chris Dunn & Ray Salas Adventure

RICK CAMERON

FOREWORD

This series of books would not have been made possible without the help of my beta readers, especially my number one fans Captain William and Maggie. Without their continuous feedback and enjoyment of these stories, these would have never been shared with you. I am also very grateful for having Ana in my life and for keeping me honest with my story telling. Her constant questioning and challenging of my semi-true stories make it all a lot more fun while I continuously answer: "keep reading". Navigating through this adventure was made much easier thanks to the guidance and suggestions of Tom Costello and Jason Price at Word Association Publishers.

CAST OF CHARACTERS

Chris Dunn – A marine biologist, scientific diver and scuba diving instructor with many years of marine search and recovery experience with a logical process personality, a go with the flow attitude individual with naval underwater demolition training.

Ray Salas – A US Coast Guard licensed captain and a long-distance swimmer with a lengthy list of mid-to-large pleasure crafts handling experience. Constantly focused on the task with a very mechanically inclined and black ops background. Always trying very hard to do the right thing.

Susana Sokolov – A Marine Biology graduate student from the Universidad de Oriente on the island of Margarita. Born in Havana, Cuba to Russian father and Cuban mother who migrated the family to Puerto La Cruz in Venezuela.

Victoria Jimenez – A Phycology graduate student from the Universidad Simon Bolivar in Caracas. Born and raised in Caracas Venezuela with a passion for the ocean. Nicknamed "Algae Girl" by her peers.

Captain Giovanni – Charter captain and an old seadog from Italian descend who had owned his boat for many years mostly chartering to sport divers in the waters of the Mochima National Park. An avid gastronome of Italian cuisine. Nicknamed "Captain Mango" by his customers.

Eduardo – Captain Giovanni's deckhand aboard the old Chris Craft Constellation.

Wilfredo and Juan – Smalltime drug runners near Puerto La Cruz, Venezuela for a powerful Colombian drug cartel.

Seaman First Class Dominguez – Venezuelan Guardacosta officer.

Petty Officer Perez - Venezuelan Guardacosta officer.

Dr. Ernesto Vargas – Director of the Laboratorio Marino Aquamarina de La Costa, an aquaculture shrimp hatchery near Santa Fe.

Dr. Rafael Bocera – Resident scientist and professor at the Laboratorio Marino Aquamarina de La Costa.

Richard (Rick) Cameron – CIA Southern Caribbean special operations specialist.

General Hernan Pineda - A retired military police general with many military and government connections in Venezuela.

Rodrigo Escalante – Drug cartel middleman stationed in Cartagena who oversees drug shipments through Mochima by Wilfredo and Juan.

Jairo – Rodrigo's right hand.

Cecilia Machado – Escalante's boss and Colombian regional cartel boss also known as "The Witch of the Mountain."

Bernardo – Cecilia Machado's personal assistant.

Buck Reilly – Owner of "The Last Resort" salvage and recoveries in Key West, Florida.

CHAPTER 1

A day after setting sail from the island of Margarita, the northeastern wind started to increase in strength in the late evening. The captain ordered the sails reefed and the deck secured. The decks of the ship were crowded with the crew tending to their duties and stations. Lines and sheets were secured, water buckets were stored below deck. The watch from the crows' nest came down the ratlines. They were moving at a slower pace than usual after many days of pillaging and debauchery in the towns of Port of Spain, Pampatar and Pueblo de La Mar. The ship had been loaded with water casks, livestock, fresh fruits, vegetables and boxes of rum for their return trip to

Kingston, Jamaica. There they would purchase a larger and newer vessel. The Christiana, a fine ship, had aged well but was tired. The captain and crew sailed her into Chaguaramas on the island of Trinidad for careening after their raid of Port of Spain. Rope and tar were used to fill gaps and leaks on her hull. Some of the rotten wood was replaced, and sails repaired before their return trip.

The ship had accumulated enough treasure in the last year that her crew agreed to sail her back to Kingston. They also agreed to make one last stop by the island of Margarita to raid the towns of Pampatar and Pueblo de La Mar (today known as Porlamar) since they were on the way to their return. Piracy was the birth of democracy. Except for when in battle or under stormy conditions, the crew could question the captain's intentions. They counted votes from the crew when plans were laid out. Most of the crew and the captain had agreed to sail to Jamaica, sell portions of the accumulated wealth to purchase a new ship and stock it.

The captain, after sighting the island of La Tortuga, ordered the helmsman of the watch to bring the ship ten degrees north. The helmsman could feel the pressure against the rudder increase. The seas were beating against the hull and water started splashing on the decks. Tired and with the idea of sailing into Kingston, the captain was reluctant to ride the coming storm protected by the island of La Tortuga, but he pushed on.

The rain started to pound the decks and the sails. While coming down from a wave a loud crack on the main mast sent pieces of wood flying onto the deck. Although repairs to the mast had been made, it wasn't strong enough to hold in the storm, even with the sails reefed. The report from the bilges was not good either. They were taking more water than they could pump out. The captain ordered to double the watch to man the pumps. A second loud crack on the mizenmast, and the wind took half of it with its rigging down. Dragging half of her mizenmast, the ship started riding up and down the monstrous waves until the rest of the mainmast folded into the water, taking the rigging and six crew members who were trying to cut the rigging of the fallen masts. The ship continued to drift south blown by the wind of the storm.

Once both masts were destroyed and hanging over into the rabid waters, it was just a matter of time before the ship turned and flipped over. The captain ordered the small boats to be put in the water to abandon the ship, but it was too late. Most of her crew couldn't swim, and those that could, would never survive the storm once in the water. The wind and the next set of waves turned the ship, taking its treasure and crew with her to the bottom of the rabid sea. There were no records of any survivors to tell the story. Word from Trinidad and Margarita had gone out about a ship of pirates raiding the coastal cities, but with very few details.

CHAPTER 2

The captain ordered the first officer to secure the decks and make the ship ready for departure. After spending three days on the loading dock of the cement factory, VENCEMOS, he had accumulated enough cement powder in his nose, lungs and mouth to last him a lifetime. He was more than ready to leave the docks of the cement factory east of Puerto La Cruz and go out to sea. He felt better when a light rain shower came over the area and washed some of the powder covering the ship, all the equipment and the crew.

The first officer came back to the bridge and reported the ship was secured for departure. The captain asked the first officer to contact the harbormaster and the dock crew for their departure. The first officer used the ship's VHF marine radio to communicate with the dockmaster. He then took a handheld radio from its charging station and gave the order to the ship's crew and the dock's crew to begin releasing the lines as he walked to the starboard wing station of the ship.

"Take us out!" the captain ordered the first officer.

"The first officer has the Com," the first officer responded.

The first officer used the bow thruster to move the bow of the boat away from the dock before using the throttles forward. The rain continued to wash the ship and the docks. Visibility was practically zero, since the first officer could not see the bow of the ship from the bridge. He was navigating using the radar for traffic and obstructions. Once the ship had cleared the docks, he turned her around in the basin and pointed her bow north. As the ship cleared Isla de La Plata, the rain increased, and the waves started to slam the starboard side of the ship. They were still on the leeward side of Isla Los Monos. The first officer suspected that the waves would increase in height once the ship cleared the island.

Many people don't realize how dangerous the cargo of cement bags is to a ship. If a stack of bags of cement moves or gets shifted during transportation, it affects the behavior of the load of the ship.

Inside one of the cargo holds, two straps holding stacks of cement bags in place snapped with the next set of waves after clearing Isla de Los Monos. The weight of the bags shifting and falling made the ship list and more water poured over the deck. The mixture of water and cement in the bilge blocked the pumps in a matter of minutes.

The bilge alarms went off on the bridge. The captain and the first officer stared at each other as the ship continued to list towards its starboard side. The first officer looked out over towards the forward deck and saw that it was too late for any other action but to abandon ship. The ship was taking a pounding from the waves over her starboard side which was almost leveled with the water.

"Give the order to abandon ship," ordered the captain as he grabbed the microphone of the marine VHF radio to call a Mayday out.

"Mayday, mayday, mayday. This is the cargo vessel Riana traveling west of Isla Los Monos. We are taking water and listing to starboard. Sinking is inevitable. We are preparing to abandon ship. Our current location is: Ten degrees, sixteen minutes and twenty-two seconds north. Sixty-four degrees, thirty-three minutes and thirty-six seconds west. Our cargo is cement. He repeated the message two more times before putting on a life jacket on, grabbing a handheld radio and a bright yellow overboard bag he always kept nearby. He walked out in the rain towards one of the lifeboats where the crew members were now gathering before boarding.

Under the torrential rain and shouting orders, the captain took a headcount and ordered the crew to put on their lifejackets and board the lifeboats. He also asked the first officer to launch two flares up into the air. Minutes after boarding and releasing the lifeboats with the entire crew, more cement bags became loosened from their pallets and more weight shifted. The ship started sinking on its side until all the air was blown out of her compartments. The one hundred- and seventy-five-foot ship Riana straightened under water and sank to the bottom of the ocean between Picuda Grande and Picuda Chica. Today, she rests on a sandy bottom and became an artificial reef after years of accumulation of sediments and marine life.

LA BORRACHA

Pico La Borracha
La Borracha
Playa el Guaro
Punta Arena,
Isla La Borracha
El Borracho

CHAPTER 3

The three screens still displayed depth at 190 feet and were still calculating bottom times for every three minutes. At 200 feet the first display flashed dashes across the screen. Chris looked around the grey and brown environment. Signaled his dive buddy and started to swim up the wall towards shallower waters. At these depths the spectrum of colors disappears because of the lack of light penetration. The brighter colors turn into dull browns and greys. The pressure compresses the tiny air bubbles of your wet suit, making it feel thinner. The mind starts playing tricks. Observations and problems take longer for the average human to process under such pressures. As they continued to swim towards their first safety stop, they could see Susana and Victoria waiting for them at the anchor at about 30 feet.

Susana Sokolov and Victoria Jimenez were graduate students from the Universidad de Oriente on the island of Margarita and The Universidad Simon Bolivar in Caracas, Venezuela. A consortium between the universities and the Mote Marine lab had been created by CARICOM for several marine projects in the Caribbean. It was a great initiative by CARICOM that started to develop future marine projects in the region. The project that had brought them together to Mochima was related to invasive species in the Caribbean and the northern coast of South America. Several sport divers had reported sightings of sea snakes and Lionfish in the waters of these islands. Previous studies had concluded that most invasive species will adapt and take over the environment for native species. Chris always had a theory associated with evolution on that subject, but those were his own thoughts on this subject.

Because of the drastic and deep incline of the waters around this beautiful national park, Chris and Ray had been contacted by a Swedish and Italian dive computers manufacturer to field test three of their newly manufactured models. The dive computers algorithms calculate bottom times every three minutes based on depth and dive bottom time. Dive computer manufacturers try to keep divers safe by turning their displays into dashes but continue to calculate bottom time and display safety stops for sport divers. The idea behind the dashes is to urge the sport divers not to continue their descend into deeper waters where they will start getting into trouble with decompression stops, that if missed will cause the Bends. The Bends is not a pretty scenario as nitrogen bubbles not released from the body will move towards articulations, most of the times shoulders and neck, making the diver walk with a bend. To cover a wide range of individuals and rates of breathing, dive computers will suggest safety stops towards the end of the dives based on the diver's bottom time.

What makes Mochima an ideal place for testing are the deep and clear waters and the dramatic rocky cliffs. With over 40 dive sites and shipwrecks available for diving all year-round, it's a sport diver's dream. Because this coast is south of the summer hurricanes path, these waters were frequented by sailboat cruisers sailing south on the eastern Caribbean and returning north via the western Caribbean. Sail boaters used to spend months in the different anchorages visiting small towns along the coast. All this until security became an issue for them and the word got out into the cruising communities with warnings to cruisers to stay clear of the coast of Venezuela. Boardings, thefts and kidnappings had been reported. These days they rather make the 400 miles crossing directly to the island of Curacao from Grenada, or the 500 miles crossing to Aruba before sailing around Bahia Hondita and southwest to Santa Marta, Barranquilla and Cartagena.

Mochima is a national park off the coast of Venezuela in the southern Caribbean. The northern coast of Venezuela has hundreds of tropical islands. Most islands extend from east to west. One of the few islands that extends north to south is La Borracha. Its name most likely derived from its opposite position and for its distance to the other islands.

Today they were diving off La Borracha. They had chartered an old 46' Chris Craft Constellation boat for the week to complete the field work around the islands of La Boarracha, Chimanas and El Faro. Once back on board after their first deep dive of the day, it was time for annotations, a change of tanks, some lunch and short discussions and comments about the dive. Susana and Victoria had no sightings of invasive species, yet. Chris and Ray compared notes and numbers from their dives while eating ham and cheese Cachitos and Frescolitas from one of the local bakeries that Captain Giovanni had brought earlier in the tender while they were loading the gear.

Giovanni was an old Italian seadog who had owned his boat for many years and mostly chartered to sport diver groups completing their advance diver certification with deep, night, wreck and navigation dives on the weekends. The boat easily accommodated twelve divers with their gear and had a small compressor and air banks to refill the dive tanks. Eduardo was Giovanni's deck hand, and he handled all the tanks and the air fills while they had lunch and prepared their gear for their second dive. The dive computers would go with them on every dive and every surface interval for the whole week and then the data was uploaded to a server in Sweden at the manufacturer plant for analysis.

After a short nap on the colorful hand-woven hammocks hung on the outer stern deck of the boat, Chris heard Ray shout from the lower dive deck: "Well Chris, are we ready for our next adventure? Let's Dive! Dive! Dive! Dive!"

Susana and Victoria were starting to gear up and buddy check their gear. After a nap, on a boat slowly swinging from side to side, it took Chris a while to come to his senses and realize where he was and what they were doing there. "I am not a morning person," he replied to Ray.

Chris and Ray had known each other for over thirty years. They had been on so many dives together and on so many boats that they very much knew what the other was thinking or acting on. Chris was the low key easy going laid back while Ray was the go, go, go from early hours of the morning. Chris always believed and told him that it was because of his upbringing around different military air bases and his Airforce family. Ray was always up by four or five in the morning working out or running before the sun was even thinking about coming up. Chris on the other hand was a night owl. His most productive times were after the sun had reached its zenith. Evening was the time when his brain kicked into turbo mode, while Ray was starting to wind down after sunset. While Ray was blond and athletic with blue eyes and a poster boy look that put girls' heads on a swivel when he walked by, Chris had black hair and brown eyes with dark skin of Latin descent. Again, complete opposites. They had met a long time ago in Miami while working for one of the marine agencies on different projects. From marsh restoration and artificial reef creation to boat deliveries and wetland restorations. As the years went by, they gained experience with the projects and before they knew it, they were in demand for different projects on different coasts and in different countries. Because of their military background along with their work they had been approached several times for collateral projects, as they liked to call them. Their marine projects were always good covers for some of the three letter agencies that requested their services.

Their second dive was much shallower than the previous one. On this dive they tagged along with Susana and Victoria to search caves and ledges around the island of La Borracha. They dove from the same location where Giovanni's boat was anchored but kept their dive to the shallower waters around the islands. It's amazing the number of crevices and small caves that exist underwater around these small islands. Most of the caves and crevices were filled with marine life; spiny lobsters, Spotted Moray eels, Top hats, Wrase, Parrots, but they did not spot any Lionfish or any type of sea snakes. While Susana and Victoria dove the western side of the island, they dove the easter side which had somewhat of a stronger current. As Chris and Ray reached their last safety stop for the dive they could see the girls at the bottom down by the anchor. Once they ascended to 15 feet, the girls climbed out onto the swim platform of the boat. When they came out of the water, there was an aroma of Italian food in the air along with the noise of the air compressor on the fly bridge. "It must be Giovanni's famous spaghetti carbonara" Chris told Ray. "I can't wait" replied Ray. "I'm starving". They rinsed their gear and suits and took Joy soap bath in salt water followed by a quick freshwater rinse.

As Chris was drying off and admiring the islands and the turquoise waters around them, the girls came over to the end of the stern deck giggling and asking if they could go on a night dive. Ray heard them and said: "I'm all out. I'm having dinner and going to sleep." Chris told them it would be fine but to be aware of the current that had turned the boat in the opposite direction from the island. "Please keep your lights on at all times while you are in the water."

They ate Giovanni's famous pasta, garlic bread and Caesar salad. By the time Chris was helping Eduardo in the galley with the dishes and silverware Ray was already looking to land on one of the hammocks with his book and the girls started to get their gear ready for their night dive. Although there was still some light, Chris saw a fast boat, what looked like a 30 or 32 Cigarette running fast behind the northern side of the island towards the Chimana islands which are the small group of islands to the east of La Borracha. The sun was already behind the horizon and the boat went by without running lights. He didn't make too much of it. Maybe the skipper forgot or has not had a chance to turn their running lights on, he thought.

"We're ready Chris!" Susana said looking up from the swimming platform.

"Remember, lights on at all times while in the water. Have fun!"

They had neon yellow Cyalume chemical light sticks attached with cable ties to the valves of their tanks so that they could keep track of each other in the event one of their lights went off.

Once they were under the water with their lights the water turned into amazing blues and greys as he followed their lights towards the inside wall of the island. As Chris took his eyes from the lights and the water and looked up, he was mesmerized by the number of bright stars and the transparency of the air in the sky. The only lights moving at a faster speed were the lights coming off the ferry heading from Puerto La Cruz to Margarita towards the southeast. A beautiful night for a night dive indeed, he thought. Chris looked at his watch to time the girls dive time and sat on one of the hammocks. Ray closed his book, looked out to sea and the tranquil waters and said: "This is another beautiful place brother!" He turned sideways towards the dark waters and was sleeping in a few minutes. As Chris looked towards the island of La Brorracha, he noticed a white strobe light but didn't make much of it. Maybe an air tower for small planes indicating the height of the island.

The air compressor finally was turned off by Eduardo and the air bled from the high- and low-pressure valves like the air brakes of an eighteen-wheeler. It all became very quiet except for the purr of the onboard generator powering the boat and charging the batteries.

Chris was in tune with the motion of the hammock and the rocking of the boat and about to doze off when he heard a distant cry calling his name. He jumped out of the hammock and walked to the end of the stern deck. About three hundred yards ahead he could see two lights floating next to each other but drifting away from the island.

"Keep your lights on!" he yelled at them with his hands cupped around his mouth, hoping that the wind would carry the sound towards them. When he turned around, Ray was already jumping on the tender. A 10-foot black rigid inflatable boat with a 25-horsepower outboard.

"I'll get them! Keep your eyes on them!" Ray said as he pulled the cord to start the outboard and proceeded to untie the painter from the swim platform.

Ray turned the tender around and headed in the direction of the lights and Chris kept his eyes on the two dots of lights slowly drifting away from the island. He also started to hear a noise he had heard earlier but could not place. The purr of the generator kept hiding the noise until it came around and he started to hear what he thought was the same fast boat he had heard earlier. He could not see it, but he heard it run towards the lights of Susana and Victoria.

Suddenly, the lights went off and Chris thought it could have been a small wave covering the lights. Then he heard the fast boat engine revving up and the noise slowly going away from them. Chris could now barely see the two lights and the running lights of the black tender approaching them. He took a breath of air thinking that Ray now had the girls on the tender.

Captain Giovanni and Eduardo joined Chris on the stern deck and as Ray approached towards the boat on the tender, Chris saw the two lights bouncing inside and the girls bright gear, but no girls.

"Where are they?" Chris asked Ray

"I don't know Chris. I found their gear floating with the lights on."

CHAPTER 4

Wilfredo and Juan had just unloaded another cargo offshore and were heading back south towards El Morro. The white strobe light on top of La Borracha would signal the "all clear" for them to make their turn towards the east once clear of the island. They had merged into the wake of the evening Ferry leaving Puerto La Cruz and bringing tourists and cargo to the Island of Margarita. Once the ferry started turning east towards Margarita they turned north out of its wake and towards their meeting point. They had to run between the islands of La Borracha and the island of Chimana for another 30 miles before the small cargo freighter would signal them to come closer and drop their cargo. Once the cargo was lifted by crane from their fast boat They turned away from the freighter and headed back.

After the strobe light on top of the island of La Borracha started signaling the three flashes for the "all clear" they relaxed a bit and made their turn. Straight ahead floating on the surface of the water were two lights moving in erratic directions.

"Juan, what do you make of that?" asked Wilfredo over the noise of the loud boat engines and the wind, pointing at the two lights.

Juan lifted his head and looked over the bulkhead. "Let's get closer! Keep the running lights off."

Wilfredo started to slow down by throttling down on the engines and pointing the bow towards the lights. As they got closer, they noticed the two divers on the surface of the water. He placed the throttles into the neutral position and the boat drifted beside the divers.

"Are you okay? Do you need help?" asked Juan bending over the gunnel of the boat.

Susana removed the regulator from her mouth shaking her head and shouted; "Yes! We got caught in the current and drifted away from the dive boat. Can you guys bring us back?" She pointed towards the Chris Craft that was now blocked by the speedboat.

Juan looked at Wilfredo with a smirk in his face and lifted one eyebrow. He turned back to the divers and said:

"Yes! Let me give you a hand. Get out of your scuba gear first so that you can climb on board."

Susana and Victoria started unbuckling their scuba rigs but kept them close to the speedboat. One by one they were helped on board, once they were seated on the stern seats of the Cigarette boat.

Wilfredo pushed the throttles forward bringing the bow higher into the air and letting it drop as the hull of the boat started to plane and gain speed. Traveling at over 50 miles per hour the girls were pinned to their seats and the wind blowing hard just over their heads. Both scuba rigs and lights just floated there on the wake of the boat.

The girls looked at each other with teary eyes, not understanding what was going on and imagining the worst.

They were now heading east between the mainland and the chain of islands of the national park of Mochima on a dark and quiet night.

Thirty-five minutes later the boat started to slow down. Wilfredo shut off the engines and the boat glided onto a cove next to another boat and two peñeros painted in different colored stripes.

It was still dark, and Juan turned around and told the girls to jump in the water before they could get a word out. Susana and Victoria looked at each other trembling from the cold water in their wetsuits and slowly slid off the side of the speedboat into waist deep water. Juan and Wilfredo followed as they started walking up to the beach towards a small fire burning inside a rock pit illuminating two more characters sitting down on the sand.

As the girls still in their wet suits approached the fire with Wilfredo and Juan behind them, one of the men sitting by the fire stood up and asked in Spanish with a very islander accent:

"Where is the shipment and who are these ladies?"

"The shipment has been delivered and these…., these are our bonuses. We found them drifting on our way back." Wilfredo looked up and down at the two girls, rubbing his hands together and then pulling black plastic cable ties from the back pockets of his pants. He tied the plastic cable ties around the girls' shaking wrists and pushed them down into the sandy beach next to the fire.

"Señoritas! Please sit down, Relax!

They started passing a bottle with liquid amber content.

BAHIA LOS COQUITOS

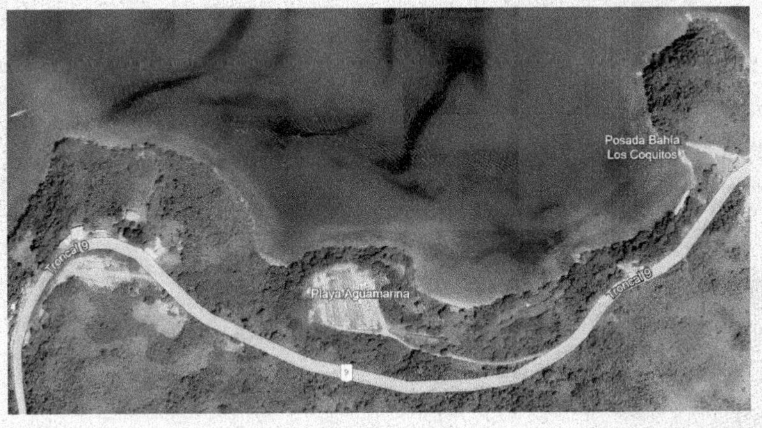

CHAPTER 5

"Captain Giovanni, contact the Guardacosta on the marine radio and the local police on your phone!" Chris said as he turned around and grabbed two underwater spotlights that had been charging with the cameras and the diving computers on the dry table.

Ray had already unloaded the girls' scuba gear and had turned the tender around by the time Chris climbed down and jumped into the inflatable dinghy.

Opening the throttle on the small outboard and getting it on plane Ray said: "I don't know what happened Chris! One minute I was looking at the lights, they disappeared for a few seconds and came back. I steered the tender directly at the lights and they were gone.

"Don't worry Ray, we'll find them. Here, take this spotlight."

They continued towards the area where they estimated the girls had disappeared and moved the lights in slow circles skimming over the water.

"Let the current take us for a bit," Chris told Ray.

They could see a blue strobe light moving from the mainland towards them at some speed. Chris also noticed for a second time a white strobe light on top of the island.

"Here comes the Guardacosta. I hope they can help," Chris said.

"They are turning east Chris! Probably looking to come up to us against the current."

In seconds a very bright spotlight from the Guardacosta came on and started circling ahead of them. They were searching for the girls on the current.

Chris turned sideways so as not to lose his night vision with the reflection of the Guardacoasta spotlight and noticed a light sheen trail on the water in the direction of the mainland but further east. The trac was not large enough to be of the ferry. "It must have been from the fast boat I saw earlier," he thought. He also started to think about the girls.

Susana with her majestic Russian- Cuban frame and blond curly hair. Susana was born in Havana from Russian father and Cuban mother. A former Russian soldier turned fisherman on the outskirts of Havana, he later moved his family to Venezuela where Susana attended graduate school at the Universidad de Oriente on the Island of Margarita. She was a water lover and passionate about the marine fauna of the area. Her interests were always in marine invertebrates. She was professional in classifying and cataloging species.

Victoria had gone to school in Caracas and was working on her postgraduate studies in phycology. We called her the "Algae Girl". Like Victoria, Caracas for some reason is the capital of the most beautiful girls on this side of the hemisphere. A mixture of old Spanish with native Indians and many generations in between had evolved to generate faces and bodies that belong on magazine covers. Victoria's black hair and her dark eyes with tan skin made her look like a princess from one of the Egyptian Mummy movies. Very mystical.

The sound of the twin engines of the small Guardacosta cutter brought him back to reality. "Where are the girls?"

Ray brought the black Zodiac tender along the starboard side of the small cutter and threw a line at one of the Seaman who tied it to a forward cleat. He climbed on board and introduced himself as Seaman First Class Dominguez. He introduced his captain as Petty Officer Perez. Perez proceeded to ask questions about the incident of the missing students but arched his brows when Chris mentioned the fast speed boat without running lights and the strobe light on top of the island. They continued at a slow speed towards the larger Chris Craft and the Seamen dropped their anchor by the side of the Chris Craft and secured fenders on the port side. Petty Officer Perez boarded behind them to speak with Captain Giovanni about the incident and seemed to get the same story and had the same reaction when Captain Giovanni mentioned the speedboat. Petty

Officer Perez explained how they would continue to search the waters further towards land but said he believed that most likely they were picked up by the speedboat.

Ray asked Petty Officer Perez his thoughts about the speedboat.His eyebrows arched again, and he started to explain that there were some drug runners in the area working the waters near Los Roques and La Tortuga from the mainland.

"There are so many coves, beaches and islands between her and the peninsula of Sucre that it is impossible to keep them guarded with the resources we have. These boats are fast and almost undetectable. They continue to change their approaches and routes which makes it much more difficult to intercept. They have labs in the mountains and move the drugs to larger boats past these islands. We will contact Captain Giovanni with any news."

The Seamen had already moved the tender around to the swim platform and boarded the small cutter. They untied the lines and brought their fenders in as they slowly backtracked their approach.

Chris and Ray were never good at the wait game. They were already thinking of scenarios and actions. They both went down into the cabins and like communicating via telepathy each one grabbed their own ditch bag and were back on the tender heading towards the mainland.

"Where do we want to start, Chris?" asked Ray like a follow up conversation that had been going on already.

"Ray, I believe we need to head towards El Morro and get on the Jeep and drive east on that coastal road number 9. Let's pay a visit to our old friend Dr. Vargas at the

Marine lab. He should be getting there in a couple of hours to monitor his hatcheries. I believe the height of the plateau where the lab sits will give us the upper hand on the view of the waters between here and the mainland. We need to find that boat."

Ray turned south towards the lights of El Morro. They rounded El Morro and entered Marina Imbuca after clearing several rock jetties which protect the marina from the northeastern seas. They tied the tender by the seawall behind a Panga, also known as a Peñero around these waters, and walked by the Marina Imbuca Dive shop. It was still dark and closed. They continued towards the parking lot of the marina and started the white jeep sitting behind the gigantic rock of El Morro with its bright light condos and hotels. They proceeded east past roundabouts, plazas and the suburbs of Lecherias.

After driving about 10 miles through empty streets in Lecherias and Puerto La Cruz, except for the newspaper trucks and one or two delivery vans, they reached the outskirts of the city and started back on coastal road 9 heading east. Another 10 miles to reach the town of Santa Fe.

Driving past the city of Puerto La Cruz, with views from the road over the port area, an abandoned refinery and the islands, while the light of dawn began to give shapes and shadows Ray asked:

"You know Chris, this is a beautiful country with vast amounts of everything. What makes it so hard to evolve into a more developed and civilized country? You see mansions and luxurious hotels, resorts, beautiful houses, and around the corner people living in very poor conditions. I don't know, it's hard for me to comprehend. It just doesn't make sense."

Chris was about to answer Ray's question when the road turned and right in front of their headlights was a military road check point. Just like they had done on their way from Caracas, they rolled their windows down as the Guarda Nacional recruits approached the jeep and started looking inside and at them.

"Papeles por favor! Asked the Guardia Nacional of not more than 18 years in age to Chris.

"What seems to be the problem officer?" asked Chris in his best Spanish that he had picked up from many Caribbean and South American countries.

"No hay problema!" answered the Guardia Nacional.

Chris turned around and reached after his ditch bag where he grabbed a small flashlight and started digging for his passport and driver's license.

Ray just sat and observed the body language of the guardias.

Chris handed his passport and his driver's license to the Guardia.

"A dónde se dirigen?"

"A Santa Fe! Científicos!" responded Chris in a neutral manner.

"Me gusta su linterna!" the guardia said to Chris while keeping an eye on the small flashlight when he switched it off.

Chris asked the guardia: "Would you like it."

The guardia looked around to make sure he was not being watched by others and slowly tilted his head up and down.

Chris handed him the flashlight and the guardia handed him his passport and his driver's license without even looking at them.

The guardia looked across the barrier and signaled the other guardia to open the roadblock for them.

"Pueden continuar," the guardia told Chris along with a hand gesture to move on.

Chris put the jeep into gear and slowly drove over the temporary bump on the road past the roadblock and into the early morning as the sun was starting to come up on the eastern horizon over the water.

"Well, Ray. To answer your question, I believe you just experienced the main reason as to why your question is a bit complicated. I am going to let Dr Vargas give you the full answer to your question."

About a mile before the entrance to the town of Santa Fe there was a curve on the coastal cliff road with a spectacular view of Coquitos Bay. Crystal clear and turquoise waters below in a cove. On the western end were the warehouse buildings of the Laboratorio Marino Aquamarina de La Costa. A productive shrimp and fish hatchery that exports larvae, small fish and shrimp to growers in the Caribbean and Panama. The hatchery has been there for many years under the supervision of scientists from different universities in the country.

On the other side of the cove, they could barely see four boats anchored and tied together very close to the beach and the bright red sand. On the western side of the cliff is Playa Colorada, named after the bright almost orange-like color of its sand.

Another half mile of cliff road and they turned left onto a gravel road that ended at a fence with cameras and two armed private guards.

Chris rolled the window down and told the guard that they were here to see Dr. Ernesto Vargas. "We are Chris Dunn and Ray Salas."

One of the guards pulled a tablet and looked at it for a few minutes while Chris noticed the shortened double barrel shot gun hanging in a holster from his belt.

The guard turned around and said: "You're not on my list of visitors. I need to call it in."

Ten minutes later the guard asked for IDs and entered their names in the visitor's log. The guard returned the IDs to Chris and walked around the jeep to write down the license plate number.

The guard signaled the other guard, and the electric gate opened enough for them to drive through it.

They drove between one of the warehouse buildings and the precipice facing the cove. Below an array of water filters, pumps and big pipes fed water from the bay up the hill into the different warehouses housing the hatcheries.

On the far side of the bay, Ray could see through the passenger window now two speedboats. The larger Cigarette speedboat and a smaller yellow and white Donzi of about 26 feet in length.

"Chris, is that the boat you saw out there?" Ray asked as he pointed towards the cove.

Chris turned and answered: "It seems like the same speedboat I saw out there. I don't know about the other one. I see some peñeros there too."

They parked at the designated visitors' parking spaces, grabbed their ditch bags, and walked towards the offices entrance of the facilities still admiring the view of the beautiful bay. They walked through a glass door and ended up facing a receptionist. Another girl that belonged on the cover of a magazine. This one with more Indian features. Shiny black hair and tanned skin.

"Mr. Dunn, Mr. Salas; Dr. Vargas is expecting you, please follow me!" The receptionist got off her chair and started walking along a series of offices all with floor to ceiling glass where you could still see the spectacular view of the small bay. She stopped at the last one and asked Chris and Ray to come in. She closed the glass door after them and left.

"Chris Dunn and Ray Salas! How long has it been? I heard you guys were playing in my backyard these days." Dr. Vargas stood up and came around his desk to shake hands.

"I tell you Doc, you have the most amazing view of this bay from your offices," said Chris shaking Dr, Vargas's hand.

"Ray! How are you? I see you are stil hanging out with this guy! How can I help you? Coffee?"

"We come seeking wisdom, but coffee would be great to start with Doc," answered Ray.

Dr. Vargas stuck his head out of the door and asked the girl at the front desk to bring some coffee in.

"The view is always there; we just get so involved with our tasks around here that we forget about it," said Dr. Vargas as he turned around and let the glass door close itself.

"I had heard from a couple of our graduate students from the UDO that you were diving the islands around here with Captain Giovanni. Sit down, sit down, please where are my manners?"

They sat around a small conference table with towers of books and files facing the bay across the glass walls. Dr. Vargas moved some of them out of the way and sat down with them.

Dr. Ernesto Vargas had a head full of greying hair and steel frame glasses that he always liked to see above them when he was asked questions. He was thin and almost athletic like. His manner had inspired knowledge and patience amongst fellow scientists in his scientific community.

Ray was the first to come back from the hypnotizing view of the bay and turned towards Dr. Vargas.

"Doc, I was just asking Chris about how such a beautiful country can be so…" his words hung there in thoughts.

"I don't know how to explain it. Not developed? Not as civilized as expected. Well, not normal? I don't know. It seems to have its own rules. Is it its history? Its culture? The geography? The temperatures? I am clueless, Doc. Please share some wisdom with us."

Dr. Vargas smiled as he looked at Ray, kept nodding his head and replied: "All or most of the above is the answer to your question, Ray".

The receptionist entered with a tray of coffees and an assortment of sugars and sweeteners, placed them on the table and left the office.

"Ray, ever since the Spanish came down here to claim these lands corruption has existed and has never left this country. The officials assigned by the Spanish crown would collect portions or commissions from boats landing here, loading, unloading, or just passing by. It was how those assigned to positions like that became rich, even from pirates, buccaneers and privateers. The officials would issue documents to privateers to capture or raid French, British or Portuguese ships but they had to bring back a cut for the government officials issuing their letters of commission.

As time went by, corruption became the norm and the culture. A couple of military dictators tried to put an end to that, but it wasn't long after they figured out that it was part of their culture and became corrupt as well. Democratic parties, Pseudo Socialist, Military Dictators, it hasn't matter throughout the years. If you have a need for a permit, a document, an ordinary ID, a passport, or just to drive through a main road, the government employees, the military, they all have a feeling of entitlement that they are to ask you for something in exchange for doing their jobs. The geography and the temperatures just make it a bit more complicated but are not the main cause. The main cause is and always has been the corruption. Oh! And it gets worse as the holidays approach, anywhere, from as soon as you land in one of the airports until the moment you step inside a plane flying out. From the leaders to the grunts. It is sad, but very true. It is indeed a beautiful country with a lot of potential in so many areas. Thirty years ago, these waters were well visited by cruisers on their sailboats and trawlers from all over the world. There was not a cove in this park where you would not find a boat anchored enjoying the views, the flora, and the fauna. Marinas and boatyards all along the coast were thriving with repairs and haul outs. It was always a good place for cruisers to haul out their boats and make repairs before they would continue their Caribbean loop. The lower labor cost and the accessibility to parts and materials made it ideal. In the last thirty years even local boaters with larger vessels have moved their boats to marinas in the Dominican Republic, Panama and Mexico. The marine industry is almost nonexistent these days. Another industry that was ran out by the lack of safety and the corruption. Younger generations don't miss any of that because they were never exposed to it. It used to be "The Place" to go and take a break if you were cruising the Caribbean, especially during the hurricane season. Most large boat manufacturers had reps or branches here. Those nice suburbs in Lecherias surrounded by canals like Pueblo Viejo and the basin of the hotel Maremares were built with the nautical industry in mind. It was going to be the Mediterranean of the Caribbean. It all came to a stop and is now another abandoned project.

The Venezuelans have a joke about when God created earth; He gave the country of Venezuela everything, gold, aluminum, oil, gas, steel, agriculture, fishing, potential for tourism, amazing mountains, beautiful beaches, snow-capped peaks, deserts, but at the end, God also gave the country the Venezuelans."

"So, as you can see, Ray, it's complicated. It's cultural Ray"

Dr. Vargas took a sip of his coffee, paused and continued:

"But corruption is like communism, it will only last until money and resources to bargain with run out. In the past two decades that has been the evolution of the country. Ever since the pseudo communist dictators calling themselves a democratic form of government took over the leadership of this country, they have run resources, enterprises, and talent out of this country. The oil and mineral business came to a halt, the large and midsize businesses pretty much left the country, along with all the professional talent. All gone, leaving a very unstable society, growing insecurity, and lacking professional services and human resources."

"Well, that's my history lesson for the day. I know you didn't come here to hear me lecture you about economics and politics. What brings you out here? Last I heard of you guys, you were on a project in Cartagena, Colombia."

Ray was deep in thought, so Chris started to explain to Dr. Vargas about the projects and research they were involved in in the area and about the missing girls.

"Doc, we're almost sure one of those speed boats down there at the other side of the bay picked up the girls while drifting with the current last night. We both saw the lights disappear for a minute or two and then reappeared when we heard the speedboat engines revved up. Do you have any knowledge of who owns the larger speedboat? The Cigarette? Where can we find them?"

"Chris, as I was explaining earlier, communism and corruption only last until funds run out. This is a typical example of the situation. Since the resources, enterprises and talent have disappeared, those that want to continue thriving must start looking for alternatives. That is where running drugs starts. We have seen it in Colombia, Peru and Mexico. The rise of drug cartels in places where there is no other economy. Those two fast boats you see down there are a small part of a drug operation that starts up in the mountains near the waterfalls of San Pedrito. San Pedrito is about six miles up the mountains on a narrow winding road."

"Our hatchery operations here suddenly are being sued by the government after over thirty years of operation. We are, according to judges bought by drug cartels, drying out a lagoon 40 miles to the west. We know we are in the way of their drug smuggling operations, and they want to run us out of this pristine location. That's the reason behind all our new security around here. We have had some unexplained incidents and mysteriously missing equipment in the last two years. Being a semiprivate funded operation with links with the best universities in the country we are an easy target for them."

"Doc," Chris interrupted Dr. Vargas. "But the place looks great! How's production?"

"We are having the highest yield and best quality in all our history of production. We export larvae and juveniles to growers in four different countries. We have weekly visits from university students from all three branches of the Universidad de Oriente. As a matter of fact, we have a group coming in this morning. We are inspiring future scientists and aqua culturists. I can sleep well at night knowing that what we do here is real."

"Chris, Ray, I'd advise you to start at sundown when these guys start loading their boats. It might be a good time to seek some answers from them. Stay here for lunch and in the late afternoon we'll walk down to the pumps and filters area by the water, and I can point out the best approach to the cove on the other side of the bay. Take part of the tour that Dr. Bocera gives our university students, and we'll meet at the cafeteria for lunch."

Chris and Ray looked at each other and Ray said: "I think it's time to go on Havana Nights Mode"

Chris immediately thought about the time they had gone into the streets of a barrio outside of Havana in the middle of a dark night to extract two agents from the hands of torturers.

"I am not good at the waiting game, but I guess Havana Nights it is then, but this time we will not be going back for your hat, Ray," replied Chris.

Chris, Ray and Dr. Vargas stepped out of the office after finishing their coffees, admiring the view and spending a few seconds looking at the speedboats at the end of the bay, then walked towards the building entrance as a group of almost thirty university students were stepping down from a grey and white bus with the UDO logo on the sides. A tall gentleman was also walking towards them from the opposite side of the building.

"Dr. Bocera!" Dr. Vargas exclaimed. "I'd like to introduce you to two very good old friends of mine. These are Mr. Chris Dunn and Ray Salas. They're working on a couple of marine related projects in the national park with some of our graduate students."

Dr. Bocera approached to shake hands with them and immediately turned to the side as the students were walking past the front glass doors. "It is a pleasure meeting you!"

"Dr. Bocera, can you include Chris and Ray in your facilities tour with the students?"

"But of course! Let's get started."

"Good morning and welcome to El Laboratorio Marino Aquamarina de La Costa! My name is Dr. Bocera but you can call me Rafa, and I will be your tour guide today. Please don't simmer on your questions as we go. Let me hear them and we'll see if we can answer them for you. We'll start towards your left with the first hatchery building."

The students turned as a disorganized group left through another set of glass doors with blue UV lights and fans followed by Chris, Ray and Dr. Bocera.

Dr. Bocera got started with his semiformal presentation: "El Laboratorio Marino Aquamarina de La Costa is a semi-private institution dedicated to the production of shrimp (*Lithopenaeus vannamei*) in different stages of growth. We have developed techniques for the hatching and growth of larvae and production of microalgae as food source for the hatcheries." Dr. Bocera went on with his presentation as he walked towards the middle of the warehouse surrounded by waist high water tanks, pipes, pumps, their noises and the students following him around.

Chris slowed down his walk and Ray got the message, private talk time.

"Ray, how come trouble has a way of finding us?" said Chris in a lower voice.

"Like a magnet! Fighting the monster, mate," replied Ray as he looked up at the clear planks on the roof allowing natural light into the tanks below.

"I need to make a phone call. I'll join you guys in a bit. See if you can round up some snorkeling gear without generating too much commotion." He walked back through the glass doors and outside of the building. From his bag he took out his satellite phone and dialed a number.

"Rick? It's Chris Dunn!"

"Chris, is this a secure line?"

"Encrypted," answered Chris.

"Go" was all that Chris heard from Rick.

Rick was one of Chris' contacts for extracurricular and/or collateral projects. From which of the three letter agencies, he wasn't sure but had a hint. Chris was brought up by diplomatic parents during the cold war and the missile crisis, so terms like secure, encrypted, coded, were not unfamiliar to him.

"Rick, what do you have on drug runners off the coast of northern Venezuela? Specifically, between Puerto La Cruz and Cumana?

"Hold" was all Chris heard. No hold music, no background noise, absolutely no noise. He waited and kept looking at the speedboats by the cove at the end of the bay as a plan started to grow in his mind. Time was not a luxury they had.

"Chris!" Rick's voice came back after four or five minutes. "It's confirmed! A cartel from the northeast mountains has been suspected of running drugs off the coast of the area to a mother ship that we have under observation. It continues under investigation since we haven't been able to identify the head and source of the cartel. We are not sure if it's of Colombian, Cuban or Mexican origin. From a source we heard they have connections in Cartagena, Colombia. Those individuals are some of our primary suspects or links. We have identified several distribution routes already. It goes without saying to proceed with caution. We have resources available near you if you need them."

"Rick, I'm not on the job," Chris interrupted.

"You are now, Chris! Smooth sailing" The phone went dead.

The next call went to another old friend, but this one closer, outside of Caracas.

"General Pineda? This is Chris Dunn. How's your health these days? How's the family?"

"Chris! How are you, kid? Long time! Health is ok, you know, not getting any younger. One day I'm marching with my platoon, the next day I'm looking at retirement. The family is doing fine. I'm a grandfather now. Can you believe it? To what do I owe the pleasure of this call?".

General Pineda was a retired military police general now for over 20 years but liked to keep his hands in the pie as he liked to say. It didn't matter whose turn or what type of government existed, he always had the right connections inside the main fort in Caracas. He had started his career right after two of the dictators that ran the country but developed the infrastructure and economics of it and had turned it over into democratic form of government that used their platforms to create what was known as the main door of South America. Immigration from all the other countries in South America had a presence in Venezuela at the time, from Argentina and Chile to Peru and Colombia. Spain and Portugal as well. It was the latter immigration that generated small companies and enterprises, making Venezuela the go to place from all other South American countries. The British, the Dutch and the Americans brought the oil exploration and production knowledge to the country for many decades. During those times you were able to sit at restaurants of a wide diversity of foods, culture and countries; European, Oriental, Middle Eastern, American. Shops, banks and stores from all over the world had branches there for their South American customers. Most airlines had a flight or a layover at the International Airport. Hotels and resorts couldn't keep up with bookings. Until the country started asking for a change. The change came, and it's still there like a parasite sucking the blood out of its host. Like an invasive species replacing the native species until they're gone.

General Pineda was always playing dominoes at parties with former presidents, congressmen, senators, ministers and private enterprise owners. He always said that scotch drinks and dominoes have always been his favorite form of making people talk and tell semi-true stories. Some of them are true and the others they don't even remember.

"General, I wanted to run something by you and find out if you have any intelligence on the subject?" Chris asked the General.

"Chris, I have been out of it for a long time, but I'll give it a try." That was his typical answer. He never committed, he never said yes or no.

"General, what have you heard on drug runners off the coast of northern Venezuela? Specifically, between Puerto La Cruz and Cumana?" Chris asked.

"Let me get back to you on that Chris! Is this a good number?"

"Yes General, thank you!" and they hung up.

Chris walked back into the building past the offices and joined the group as they were exiting the rear of the building into another long warehouse with a similar layout of pools and pumps. He didn't see Ray walking with the group of students and didn't make a big deal of it either.

Once inside the second building Dr. Bocera continued with his explanations and answering questions for the students about nutrients, growth rates, parts per thousand and parts per million. Chris's mind kept wandering to the girls, Susana and Victoria, until Ray walked behind him and asked.

"Gathering intelligence?"

"Confirmed!" answered Chris, as if they were reading each other's thoughts.

"Gear?" asked Chris.

"Lined up!" answered Ray.

They both merged with the group and ended up in the cafeteria where Dr Vargas sat at a table waiting for them.

Yellow rice with chicken, fried plantain and garden salad with natural watermelon juice was the lunch menu of the day. They ate, drank, and made small talks about projects, people, politics, economy, the usual, new and old. Some of the students were on their phones, some were reading material they had gathered or was distributed to them.

"Okay ladies and gentlemen, two more buildings to go. Keep the questions coming," shouted Dr. Bocera over the noise of the students. The students stopped what they were doing and gathered towards the entrance of the next building.

Chris and Ray decide to sit a bit longer after the students left until Dr. Vargas stood up from the table placed, his tray on a cart with the other trays and said:

"Ray, come with me."

Ray stood up, and Chris said: "I've a few more calls to make. I'll hang around here."

Once Dr. Vargas and Ray were gone, Chris called Captain Giovanni for an update. He had no news from the Guardacosta or the local police. The girls' phones kept ringing but he didn't want to touch them, much less answer them. Chris asked Captain Giovanni if he would be so kind as to move the boat to Playa Puinare on the island of Chimana Grande and that they would meet him there with the tender later tonight or in the morning. Giovanni was eager to move and get busy. Chris again asked him to keep him informed with any news or changes.

Chris walked back towards the offices and from a far saw Ray leaving Dr. Vargas' office with a large black bag and out the glass doors. A few minutes later he joined them in Dr. Vargas' office.

"Let's walk down to the shore where the water pumps are," Dr. Vargas said.

They left the office building, walked across the parking area and down the concrete steps to the bottom of the cliff where an array of saltwater pumps, pipes and filters were concealed inside perforated block walls for ventilation. These pumps and pipes brought water from the bay up the hill to the aquaculture hatchery above. Chris looked up towards the buildings. They were at least ten stories high from the beach. Looking down beside one of the block buildings, he noticed the large black bag Ray was carrying earlier out of the building.

Dr. Vargas briefly explained the pumping process and turned around towards the east end of the beautiful bay. The calm turquoise waters against the bright red sand looked like a postcard or a vacation brochure. The sun was starting to drop closer to the horizon on the west side. The soft and lazy waves echoing against the cliff behind the beach sounded like the background of a Caribbean song. They saw a few kids swimming and playing on the beach but no one else. Towards the north three miles out across the gulf of Santa Fe, they could see the west end of the Sucre peninsula and La Morena beach.

Turning around Chris said: "This might be a good time to get started and position ourselves for the party."

Dr. Vargas nodded and shook hands with them saying: "Let me know if there is anything else you need. I will make security aware that you are driving back out later. I'll be back here in the morning in case you get delayed. Good hunting, gentlemen!"

They said their goodbyes and Dr. Vargas slowly climbed back up the steps as Chris and Ray sat on the red sand and prepared the gear for a swim. Ray pulled out of the bag two pairs of large skin-diving fins that require a slower and wider kick but were very effective.

"Where did you find these?" I asked Ray.

"Loaners from Dr. Vargas. He has a large dive gear locker, compressor and first aid facilities up there," Ray replied.

"It's having old friends like Dr. Vargas that you can count on to make this world a better place. He has never asked for anything in returned," Chris commented.

"I'm starting to worry about time and the girls. It's been over eighteen hours since we lost track of them. I know they are strong, but they could use our help too. The more time goes by the harder it will be to get to them. I'm worried more about human trafficking than anything else," Ray said.

"Let's prepare that welcome party," Chris said to Ray.

"I'd feel a lot better with a rum and coke in one of my hands this time of the evening instead of a mask, fins and knife," replied Ray.

"Semantics," Chris said as he moved slowly towards the clear cool water of the bay, observing the beach and estimating the distance to the cluster of boats anchored on the other side.

Chris placed the mask over his head and slipped the long black fins on. Hyperventilating and with a slow and smooth motion he started swimming underwater towards the cluster of boats. He had heard Ray walking into the water behind him, but then lost track of him in the darkness.

SANTA FE

Playa Santa Fe
Mercado Municipal "Santa fé"
Estadio de Beisbol
Playa Cochaima
Troncal 9
Sta Fe
Playa Aguamarina
L.B. Mariano de la Cova
Santa Fé
La Gracia de Dios
ada Los
s del Valle
José pinto

CHAPTER 6

Susana and Victoria had been pushed up the hill in the dark and into the back of an old faded blue rusted hardtop Toyota Land Cruiser FJ40 that was parked along the side of the coastal road facing Coquitos Bay on the Gulf of Santa Fe. They sat face to face on the rear side benches shaking from the cold water in their wetsuits and from the near future expectations. They were both thinking the worst.

Wilfredo started the beat-up Land Cruiser FJ40, and headed east on the coastal road towards Santa Fe while Juan sat in the passenger seat with his right arm hanging out of the window. Every few minutes Juan turned his face to keep an eye on the girls. They drove for a mile on the outskirts of the town of Santa Fe and up a narrower and less maintained road towards the mountains. They drove past the village of El Naranjo where small houses hugged the road. Climbing another three miles they entered the small village of San Pedro. Susana and Victoria were not aware of their whereabouts now. They had never been up these mountains. Green ferns, yellowish and green moss and small trees got denser as they drove higher into the mountains.

Five minutes beyond the village of San Pedro, Wilfredo made a turn into a dirt road that crossed over a shallow river and led to caves and waterfalls. He drove on to the rocks under a couple of waterfalls and stopped inside one of the dark, high caves.

"Get out!" Juan told the girls as he opened the back doors of the old Land Cruiser.

Wilfredo walked ahead of the girls, Juan behind, and they turned towards a smaller cave where there was a fire lit at the center. Two more men sat around it smoking what smelled like burning weed, which they shared with the others.

Juan pushed the girls to the ground near a corner of the cave and sat down by the fire with Wilfredo and the other two.

"We need to get out of these wetsuits," Susana said to Victoria, almost a whisper.

"I'm not sure I want to be in my bathing suit around these gorillas," mumbled Victoria.

"Be quiet!" yelled Juan from the center of the cave. The sound carried against the walls.

Half an hour later Wilfredo stood up on wobbly legs and told the others he was driving down to buy more rum and to check on the boats. Turning around looking at the girls he said:

"Don't start the party without me."

"What do you want to do with them?" Juan asked Wilfredo

"We'll have ourselves a nice party tonight and then we'll dump them on the ship for the Mexicans to do with them whatever they want. We'll take them out with the next load before the boss comes back for the next inspection. We can't let him see them. He doesn't like to deal with used merchandise, and they will be used by the time we're done with them.

Wilfredo left the larger cave and walked back to Land Cruiser and drove back past the waterfalls and down the mountain road.

SAN PEDRO

Playa
Cochaima
San Esteban
Santa Fé
Playa Piscina
Playa Los
Hicacos
el naranjo
Playa Pescador
Playa Colorada
Playa Arapito
ARAPO
San Pedrito
Cascadas de San Pedro
Iglesia, Altos De Sucre
Los Altos
de Sucre
San Pedro

CHAPTER 7

Chris barely surfaced the water two times before reaching the cove with the cluster of boats on the other side of the bay. Slowly and silently, he turned his head to the sides trying to find Ray, not a sight. The children on the beach were gone and it was very quiet in the cove. Only the slapping of water from the small waves. With a smooth, almost fluid motion, Chris climbed the stern of the Cigarette boat, crawled over the engine cover and onto the carpeted deck. He lifted his head to look inside the next boat anchored by the side and saw a familiar face. Ray was laying down on the stern seat of the Donzi with a smirk on his face. They both turned towards the beach when they heard an engine driving into the parking area above and was shut off followed by the slam of a door. Chris gave Ray an acknowledgement nod and laid down on the deck of the boat behind the passenger front seat. The deck carpeting was wet, moldy with a never-had-been-dry smell. It was definitely a very old model. Maybe from the era of the Cocaine days of South Florida.

Now Chris could hear someone coming down the steps of the cliff and splashes in the water. He waited until Wilfredo started climbing on the port side of the sleek boat and grabbed Wilfredo by the shirt neck and his belt throwing him onto the carpeted deck. Ray immediately jumped from the other boat and landed on the cushioned engine cover of the old Cigarette boat. They grabbed Wilfredo by his arms and sat him down on the stern seat.

"We need to have a conversation right here right now!" Chris glared at Wilfredo.

Wilfredo was just getting over his weed and rum induced high with a headache from the long day and evening. His headache worsened as he looked back and forth between Chris and Ray.

"What do you want? You're not allowed aboard this boat," said Wilfredo with wide eyes.

"The two girls scuba diving that you picked out from the water, where are they?" asked Chris.

Ray turned around and started looking into compartments for docking lines. In one he found some quarter inch lines with a lot of mildew and colorless.

"Lay down on your belly," Ray ordered Wilfredo and proceeded to tie his hands behind his back with one of the lines.

Both Chris and Ray lifted Wilfredo to his feet and pushed him in the water. Wilfredo struggled and Chris followed him by jumping over the side of the boat. Ray went back to the locker and grabbed two more lengths of docking lines before jumping over the side of the boat.

In between the two boats they walked out of the water towards the beach looking from one side to another for spectators. There were none. They climbed the rudimentary steps up to the cliff and walked towards the old Toyota Land Cruiser.

"Keys!" Ray demanded of Wilfredo.

"Inside my right pocket," Wilfredo answered in a low tone.

Ray searched his pockets and found the keys and a pocketknife. He put the pocketknife inside one of his short pockets.

Chris opened the rear doors and pushed Wilfredo up inside the rear noticing the wet floor of the cabin. Ray locked the rear doors after Chris had closed them.

"What's your name?", Chris asked Wilfredo as he got on the passenger side of the land Cruiser and sat sideways facing the driver seat.

"Wilfredo," he answered with the same low tone and not knowing where he was going to end.

Chris explained to Wilfredo: "Wilfredo, this ride has two stops. The first one will stop at the place where the girls are. The second you will never come back from. Which one will it be?"

Wilfredo turned and looked at Ray as he climbed into the drivers' seat. Then he turned back to look at Chris undecided about his answer.

"You don't know who you're messing with. I'm just a delivery guy. The girls, well, the girls, um…

Chris turned and reached back to grab Wilfredo by his shirt and said:

"We don't care about anything else but the girls. Where are they?" Chris asked, pulling Wilfredo towards him. "Where do you want to end up?"

"Okay mi pana! Okay! They are up on the hill by the waterfalls," Wilfredo replied with fear in his eyes.

Chris just pushed him back and asked Ray to start driving towards Santa Fe as he searched the glove compartment in front of him. There he found a lighter, an old roll of duct tape, spare light bulbs and a bunch of old paper.

They drove past Playa Cochaima which was lined up with anchored peñeros along the beach and turned staying on the main road into Santa Fe. They drove past a Guardia Nacional post but the guardias didn't even get up from their card game recognizing the old Land Cruiser. Once clear of Santa Fe they made a right turn into the Camino Viejo Road and started climbing towards El Naranjo. Chris kept turning and asking Wilfredo for directions.

Past the town of El Naranjo, Wilfredo told them to turn into a smaller road to the right and they started heading west towards San Pedro on a dirt road. It was another dark night, but they could still see the vegetation changing under the reflection of the lights. The tropical coast vegetation turned mountainous and wet. Ferns and moss covered the rocks on the side of the road. The smell of coastal area changed dramatically into mountain air. The change in temperature was also noticeable. After another two miles they started to see houses on the side of the small road in the town of San Pedro.

As they reached the end of the town, Chris turned towards Wilfredo.

Resigned, Wilfredo said: "Take the next dirt road on the left"

Ray turned into a dark dirt road. The lights of the town of San Pedro no longer in view, and suddenly, a river running downhill was all he saw under the headlights. Ray stepped on the brakes and the Land Cruiser slid on the dirt road to a stop.

Chris turned around to look at Wilfredo with a menacing stare.

"Is this one of your tricks? Or you prefer the freshwater of a river?"

With a smirk, Wilfredo said: "Drive through it. It's shallow here. Do you see how the road continues the other side of the river?"

Ray slowly started driving forward and getting a feel for the behavior of the vehicle as they entered the water which ran in one direction. As they moved forward the water almost reached the top of the tires, but they continued to the other side. The Land Cruiser slipped as it came out of the river but then the tires grabbed the pebbles and rocks and climbed back onto the dirt road. They continued climbing up the road. The rocks kept getting bigger and suddenly they were driving on solid boulders towards several waterfalls. Ray could barely see the worn rocks by the tires going under a waterfall and inside a cave where the tracks ended. He stopped the Land Cruiser and shut it off. It was dark, but they could see a faint light coming from inside of the cave.

Chris and Ray stepped out onto the wet rocks. Chris grabbed the roll of duct tape from the glove box and Ray walked around and opened the rear doors. Chris pushed Wilfredo back, climbed into the cabin, placed a piece of the duct tape on Wilfredo's mouth and stepped back out.

"Lock it," he said to Ray as he closed both doors to the rear cabin.

The faint light coming from the interior of the cave seemed to emanate from a fire. Chris and Ray walked slowly towards the flickering light. There was a turn at the end of the main cave, and they now could see a fire burning inside a second cave. They stopped and could see someone sitting by the fire. Another man was standing to the side of the cave saying something to two more people sitting in the dark.

"I'll go right, you go left. Give me a 5 second head start," Chris told Ray over the noise of the waterfall on the other side of the parked Land Cruiser.

Chris started walking towards the fire, the guy sitting by the fire raised his head and said: "You're back! We are out of rum."

Five seconds later Ray was blind punching the side of the head of the other guy standing by the girls. He fell immediately to the ground completely lights out. Ray took the pocketknife out of his pocket and started cutting the plastic ties from Susana's and Veronica's wrists when he heard a shot fired and turned to see Chris standing up from the ground over the guy by the fire.

The girls yelled and ducked under the sound of the gun bouncing off the rocks inside the cave. Ray jumped and in two very long steps was standing by the fire to see Chris picking up the gun from the other guy sprawled on the ground.

Chris had jumped over the fire pit and had landed on top of the man's hand while he was trying to go for the gun. It was then that a shot was fired by the guy when Chris had stepped on his hand. Chris's other foot was planted on the guy's face as part of the momentum.

With all the commotion, they hadn't noticed a third smaller cavern to the side. Chris and Ray looked at each other. The girls were getting out of their wetsuits. Chris and Ray looked back at the next cave and started walking towards it. What they saw inside was the monster.

The third cave was a deposit of prepackaged cocaine. Some were ready to be transported in waterproof pouches. Others were waiting to be bundled and packed.

Ray whistled and said: "The Mother Load!"

They walked back out to see the girls now in their bathing suits getting warmed up by the fire.

Ray tied the hands of the two unconscious guys that were now turning and moaning. One of them was asking for Wilfredo when Ray saw a shadow run out of the cave towards the waterfall. Chris was already running behind the third guy, but he jumped down into the river.

Chris walked back and said: "That one ran like rabbitfish!"

At this point the girls were crying and hugging Ray. Susana and Victoria hugged Chris in tears and were very thankful. They looked exhausted and cold.

Chris asked them: "Are you ladies, okay? Any cuts or bruises? We need to get you some clothing or blankets. It's cooler up here in the mountains."

The girls shook their heads and Victoria said: "We're just glad you came. "

Ray was lifting one of the guys from the ground and Chris went to lift the other one. They walked them out of the cave followed by Susana and Victoria. They sat the guys down behind the curtain of water from the waterfall above and the girls took advantage of the falling water to rinse themselves of the salt water they were carrying since they had been picked up by the speedboat.

Ray went to get Wilfredo out of the rear cabin of the Land Cruiser while Chris yelled over the noise of the waterfall: "I'll be right back."

Chris walked back inside the main cave towards the fire and grabbed a couple of logs that had been recently placed inside the pit but were already burning. He walked inside the smaller cave and placed the burning logs on the ground in each corner of the piles. It didn't take long for the cave to become a small burning inferno.

"There goes the monster," Chris thought to himself and walked back outside.

Ray had seated Wilfredo next to the other two guys behind the falling water and was helping the girls climb inside the rear cabin of the old Toyota FJ40.

Chris walked by the three guys and shouted over the falling waters: "Buena suerte!"

Wilfredo shouted back what sounded like: "You don't know who you're messing with."

Ray turned the Land Cruiser around behind the waterfall and started the climb down from the rocks into the dirt road as Chris jumped onto the passenger seat and closed the door. In the rearview mirror he could now see a brighter reflection of the fire inside the caves.

"You sure know how to make and exit,"

They crossed the river and were back on the dirt road on the opposite side heading down the mountain.

"How are we doing?" Chris asked, turning around to see the girls hugging each other and shaking. The girls agreed they were fine.

They started to see the small houses along the road of San Pedro when Chris said:

"Stop and turn the lights off."

Chris jumped out of the car still moving and quietly walked towards the side of a house. He jumped a short wall separating the road from the front patio and pulled something hanging on lines from the side of the house. He ran and jumped back in the Land Cruiser.

Chris turned around and handed two blankets to Susana and Victoria while saying:

"It's not L.L. Bean, but it will do for now. At least until we get back down to the coast."

Ray continued downhill turning the headlights back on after a couple of blocks down the narrow road past San Pedro and the town of El Naranjo.

The light of the morning could be seen over the waters below by the time they drove to the crossing with the main road. Fatigue, thirst, and hunger were starting to settle into all four of them after the whole ordeal. Ray saw a place still lit up right in front with a sign advertising as Panaderia and Pasteleria La Reina de Santa Fe. He turned and pulled over to the side of the main road, stopped the car and said: "I'll be right back."

After ten minutes Ray walked to the passenger side window and handed Chris a small carton tray with four cups of coffee and a bag of pastries. Another bag contained four small cartons of orange juice.

Ray said: "It's not Continental but will do for now, as Chris rolled the window down and accepted the tray and the bags.

"How'd you pay for all this?" Chris asked

Ray pulled a credit card out his pocket and said: "Plastic! Never leave home without it."

Chris smiled wondering what else Ray carried in all his cargo short pockets.

CARTAGENA

La Boquilla
Santa Rosa
Villanueva
Pradera
Cartagena
Isla de Tierra
Bomba'
Turbaco
Mamonal
Pasacaballos
Arjona
Pendales
90B
90
Barú
El Viso
Puerto Badel

CHAPTER 8

Rodrigo Escalante was having breakfast by his private pool on the top floor of his building at the southern tip of Castillo Grande, a suburb of Cartagena facing the Bay. Rodrigo liked Cartagena. It was a city with a lot of history of the old Spanish empire, pirates and buccaneers, particularly the Bay of Cartagena. It had been set up by the Spanish Armada as a stronghold and became one of the main trading ports for Spain. Cartagena, because of its trading port, had also been raided several times by famous pirates back in the days of piracy.

The bay of Cartagena has two openings into the Caribbean; Boca Grande, which is the widest opening, but it's blocked with a wall of coral rocks that tricked the British Royal Navy and pirate ships by running aground into the wall when trying to enter the bay. The second and smaller opening is called Boca Chica, where two garrisons were built on each side with huge chains that could be lifted and lowered in the water column. When under chase from the enemy, the Spanish Armada and trading vessels would go through into the bay and the chains were then lifted from the bottom to stop the pursuing vessels. Once the enemy vessels were stopped by the chains, they would be fire upon them with cannons from the fort named Fuerte de San Fernando. It was also a very strategic place to be for Rodrigo Escalante because of the many exits Cartagena provided him. He could always escape by boat to the south, by plane to the north and by car to the east in case he needed to.

The tourists, the heat and the noise that traveled over the waters of the bay were some of the things Rodrigo disliked about Cartagena. The mountains were cooler and quieter, but more difficult to run his business from. The airport in Cartagena was small enough that he could buy his way through. His cartel always had the right insiders in strategic places at the main port across the bay and the naval base and academy were too busy and broke trying to keep their submarines and cutters afloat under the eye of the government heavyweights in Bogota.

He was interrupted by one of his lieutenants, as he liked to call them so he wouldn't call them Grunts.

"Jefe, con permiso?"

"Si Jairo! I don't know why they wear these bikinis nowadays. They might as well walk around naked." Rodrigo said referring to the two girls lying face down on lounge chairs across the pool playing Ballenato music out of a speaker. They were barely 18, if that.

"Jefe, we 're having problems in Mochima. Some Gringos burnt half of the shipment before it was brought out to the ship and left our boys tied up by the waterfalls earlier this morning. I just received a call from Wilfredo." Explained Jairo.

"Call Sableta and tell him to get the plane ready. We'll leave in two hours" said Rodrigo standing up and throwing the napkin on top of his unfinished breakfast. He gave Jairo a stare, shouted out to the girls that he would be back later and walked inside through glass doors towards his bedroom.

CHIMANA GRANDE

CHAPTER 9

The sun was coming out over the horizon by the time they were driving back on the coastal road out of Santa Fe bordering Playa Cochaima. Now not so hungry and thirsty but still very tired they approached the gates of the Aguamarina de la Costa lab and hatcheries. It took a few minutes for the private guards to allow them past the gates, they parked the Land Cruiser next to the Jeep and got out stretching their bodies under the morning sun and facing the beautiful bay of Los Coquitos.

Chris looked across the bay towards the speedboats and said to Ray: "Get the girls some clothing from Dr. Vargas if you can, and head back to the marina at El Morro. Get on the tender and go out to Playa Puinare on the Island of Chimana Grande. I'll meet you on Giovanni's boat."

Chris grabbed his ditch bag from the Jeep and climbed on the drivers' side of the Land Cruiser. He was about to drive out of the aquaculture complex when he saw Dr Vargas driving an old midsize pickup truck past the gates towards him. He stopped and rolled the window down to speak with Dr. Vargas.

"Good morning!" Dr. Vargas said from the cabin of the pickup truck.

"Good morning, Dr. Vargas!" Chris replied.

"I can see you had a productive field trip last night!" said Dr. Vargas looking straight towards the Jeep where Ray was standing with Susana and Victoria.

"Very productive indeed, Doctor" Chris said.

"Is there anything else I can help with?" Dr. Vargas asked.

"Doc, do you happen to have some clothing you can supply the girls with for the trip back to the boat? Maybe from your students lost and found pile?

"Not a problem! We have plenty to choose from" replied Dr. Vargas.

Chris then told Dr. Vargas: "I must run an errand and then head back out to Chimana Grande. We'll bring your snorkeling gear in a couple of days before driving back to Caracas.

Dr. Vargas waved his hand, started driving and parked next to the Jeep.

Chris continued past the security gates and turned left back towards the other side of the bay. He parked the Land Cruiser and took his phone out. He had missed several calls and messages on his satellite phone. His first call went out to Rick, his contact at the three-letter agency for which he had no clue which three letters. He punched the number from memory.

"Rick! Chris Dunn."

"Secured?" Rick replied from the other end.

"Encrypted" replied Chris.

"I heard you had fun last night!" Rick said.

"Gossips travel faster than ever these days" Chris replied.

"They do, and now you're committed whether you like it or not. Our project just jumped to the next level. You have our total support, land, air and sea" Rick said.

"Great!" was all Chris could come up with.

"Listen, we have identified one of the heads down in Cartagena. Rodrigo Escalante likes to travel light between private airstrips in Colombia and Venezuela. He's been landing and taking off from a private strip south of the cement factory, which is only 10 miles from where you are now. Intelligence places him in route from outside of Cartagena, Colombia. He should be there by late morning today."

"Rick, I'm tired from a long night and I'm not thinking straight. I will call you later today before I say something that I will later regret" and he hung up.

Chris also had a call from General Pineda and from Captain Giovanni. He called Captain Giovanni next.

"Captain Giovanni, Chris Dunn!"

"Hey Chris! We're still anchored at Playa Puinare as you requested" responded Captain Giovanni.

"Excellent Captain! Ray and the girls should be arriving in a couple of hours with the tender. I will not be far behind" Said Chris.

"We'll sit tight Chris! God speed!" Captain Giovanni said, and he hung up.

Chris got out of the Land Cruiser and checked that all the doors were locked. He walked down the steps to the beach and climbed into the larger speedboat. He started opening every box and every compartment until he found the set of keys on cutoff lanyards. He took the Land Cruiser's keys and threw them in the same small box where he had found the boat keys. He walked back towards the engine cover and lifted it on its air shocks to let air in and out. He went back to the drivers's side and started the twin 520HP Mercruiser Racing Engines. Chris walked back to the engine cover and closed it. Checked the fuel gauges and then turned the windlass on and lifted the anchor from the bottom. He reversed the boat out of the cove slowly and trimmed the lower units as he turned the boat around pointing its bow towards the west. Up on the hill he could see the white Jeep heading west too. He revved up the engines halfway up the throttles. Within seconds the bow came out of the water and the boat dropped on a plane cruising at over forty miles per hour.

He slowly approached Captain Giovanni's Chris Craft letting him know it was him tying up against the port side. Eduardo hung fenders from the handrail low enough for the speedboat not to bump into the hull of the Chris Craft. Chris grabbed his ditch bag and climbed up to the deck to greet Captain Giovanni.

"Good morning, Captain!" Chris said. "Eduardo, thanks for the fenders!"

"Good to see you too Chris!" said Giovanni in his always happy tone. "Where are Ray and the students?"

"They'll be here in a few. They were driving to Marina Inbuca to bring the tender back." Said Chris

"Captain, you do have radar and AIS on this boat, right?" asked Chris to Captain Giovanni.

"Yes, on the radar, half a yes on the AIS. I don't like to transmit a signal, only receive. You know, with the lack of security and law enforcement around here I'm not inclined to show everyone where I can be found. Follow me to the bridge."

Eduardo secured a stern line to the Cigarette boat and Captain Giovanni climbed the ladder to the bridge. Chris followed.

"What are we looking for, Chris? Radar and AIS are on right now" said the Captain.

Chris started explaining: "I am looking for a ship out here no more than 10 miles offshore, not too big, but small enough to go unnoticed or mixed up with boat traffic in the area. Not a Panamax class, a smaller cargo ship. Inter-island trader most likely, with one or two derricks."

"Let's see what we have out there Chris!" the captain said, as he turned a display on the bridge with green, red and blue arrows pointing in different directions.

"Here is the NOAH. It's a Cargo/Containership and is sailing under the flag of Antigua Barbuda. Her length overall is 148 meters, and her width is 23.28 meters. It's heading to Guanta."

"No, I don't think so. That might be too big" said Chris.

"Here is another one; The Anita, but it's a crude oil tanker under Tanzania flag heading to Punta Cardon."

"No, not a tanker," said Chris. "What's the blue arrow over here about fifteen miles north of Playa Colorada?"

Captain Giovanni clicked on the smaller blue arrow and to their surprise, the ship was not transmitting and was out of coastal range.

"That's the one I'm looking for, Captain. See if you can get more details on it."

Chris called Rick and asked him for details of the ship and its location which he received in the form of a link in a text message. He clicked on the link and all the information appeared. The ship name was the Tzini under a flag from Malta. It was a Class A Cargo/Hazard containership with length overall of 170 meters and width of 29.8 meters.

On a separate note, Rick wrote: "That is the same fish we have been observing. It doesn't transmit origin, destination nor speed. It has been cruising 10 miles west and 10 miles east in the area for the last five days."

"Chris, I don't want to sound the alarm here, but there is another one of those speedboats heading straight at us. You can see it here, the yellow arrow pointing at us about 15 miles east" Captain Giovanni said with some excitement in his voice.

Chris saw the yellow arrow on the display, indicating a speedboat not transmitting but on a direct approach towards them from the east. He thought about the Donzi boat that was anchored next to the Cigarette speedboat in the cove, He looked up and noticed the black tender approaching from the west with Ray, Susana and Victoria.

"Thank you for your help, Captain!" Chris said.

"What are you going to do, how can I help?" asked the captain, as Chris was starting to climb down the ladder back to the main deck.

"It's better that you don't know Captain. Please feed the girls and make sure they call their relatives to tell them that they're okay. Also let the Guardacosta know that they're okay" shouted Chris as he landed on the deck.

"How was your trip?" Chris asked Ray and the girls, now wearing different attire. They climbed out of the tender into the swim platform below.

Eduardo was tying the tender to the starboard side of the boat as soon as they had all stepped on the platform.

"New acquisition?" Ray asked pointing at the speedboat.

"No, we have company coming. I am thinking of a search and destroy party, want to go?" asked Chris after the girls had climbed the ladder to the main deck to greet the captain.

"Let's party brother! But you do know that there is no prosecution, judges or juries around here that you can present a case to without buying them, right? asked Ray.

"Well, there is that too, but we're going black ops this time. Do you remember that old cargo ship full of concrete bags, that left the cement factory VENCEMOS on the outside of Puerto La Cruz and never made it past the islands?" Chris asked Ray.

"Yeah, yeah, the cement boat they call it, we dove there several times" said Ray.

"Let's go and get some coordinates from Captain Giovanni" Chris said, as he started to climb the steps up to the bridge.

"Captain Giovanni, we need your help again" said Chris, as he entered the bridge with Ray.

"How can I help" asked the captain.

"A couple of things, first, we need coordinates for the cement boat wreck between Isla Picuda and Isla El Faro. Second, I need you to give me a heading over the marine VHF radio from the cement boat to where the TZINI is sitting when I call you. Can you help us with that without getting more details?" Chris asked the captain.

Captain Giovanni turned around and picked up a small notebook and a pen and copied the latitude and longitude numbers from the chart plotter screen and gave it to Chris saying: "I'll be standing by on channel 16 and 78. Call me on 78 for the heading when you need it."

"Thank you, Captain! Can you write the coordinates again for Ray?" Chris asked.

Captain Giovanni turned around and copied the co-ordinates to the cement boat wreck again and handed it to Ray. "Here you go Ray! Good luck with whatever it is you're doing gentlemen."

Chris and Ray climbed down the steps back to the main deck. Chris started loading his scuba gear into the speedboat tied on the port side of the Chris Craft. Before boarding, Chris asked Ray for a 10-minutes head start, and then asked Eduardo to untie the speedboat from the Chris Craft. Chris started the twin Mercruiser engines and backed out of Playa Puinare and headed east between

Chimana Grande and Chimana del Este islands. Once clear of the islands, he revved up the engines and got the boat on a plane going about 50 miles per hour. Isla El Faro went by very fast on his port side, and almost immediately Cachicamo was on his starboard side. He pulled out the piece of paper with the coordinates for the cement boat wreck. It only took him a short time to complete the ten-mile trip and reach the wreck site. He looked up, and in the distance towards the southeast he could barely see the orange Donzi speedboat heading towards him.

Once on top of the wreck, he opened the engine cover and with a knife cut a couple of hoses coming out of sea-cocks in the hull of the boat. Water started gushing into the bilge. He closed the engine cover and lifted his SCUBA gear up to the bench seat and buckled it, slipped into his fins and put his mask around his neck. He called Captain Giovanni for a heading and used the speedboat compass to point the bow and tie a line from the steering wheel to the bottom of the bucket seat. He wasn't sure if this was going to work. He then sat with his legs over the side of the boat and in a single motion pushed the throttle all the way down and jumped in the water as the boat slipped under him and gained speed.

Chris immediately dove underwater towards the cement boat wreck clearing his mask of water and compensating for the air inside his ears by moving his jaw left to right. The cement boat wreck appeared before his eyes. He could see all the cement bags without their paper, some stacked and some just laying around on top of the wreck. Except for the algae, coral growth and fish, it hadn't changed much from the last time he was there. He swam towards the bow of the wreck and sat on top of the large windlass to wait for Ray to pick him up on the tender. He heard the Donzi speedboat go by above on the surface and with a smile pictured the drug smugglers chasing their own boat out to sea.

Ray started to slow down the tender after clearing Isla Cachicamo. He was lining up his approach towards the wreck site of the cement boat. A few minutes later he saw Chris surface and headed towards him at idle speed. When he reached Chris, he shut off the outboard and helped Chris with the SCUBA gear.

Chris kept his mask and fins on and kicked himself up on the side of the tender. When he took his mask off, there was a loud sound, but far away, almost like thunder. Chris and Ray looked at each other with mischievous smiles.

Ray said: "Maybe it's time for rum and cokes my friend."

"Let's hope so!" It was all that Chris could say at this point, exhaustion was starting to settle in after two straight days on the run.

Ray turned the outboard on and pivoted the tender around back towards the Chimana islands and Playa Puinare.

Over the sound of the wind and the small outboard motor Ray said to Chris: "You do know we just started a small war, right? This doesn't end here."

"I know!" replied Chris. "This might have been childish and stupid on my side, but I hate bullies and drug runners in that order. So, we find ourselves fighting the monster

again" Chris continued and stared out towards the beautiful islands of the park.

When Chris and Ray returned to Captain Giovanni's
Chris Craft and unloaded the tender, Chris went straight
for a freshwater shower and turned around to land on
one of the hammocks hanging in the shade of the main
deck. Two minutes later with the adrenaline fading he
was lights out.

CHAPTER 10

Rodrigo Escalante took a shower, got dressed in a light color suit, a black shirt without a tie and headed down in his private elevator to the parking garage on the first floor of his building. Standing there holding the rear door of a refitted bulletproof Nissan Armada was Jairo, his lieutenant.

"Siga Jairo, siga!" was all that Rodrigo said, as he climbed into the back seat of the Nissan SUV.

"Vamos Lucho!" Rodrigo told his driver.

Jairo barely had time to jump on the passenger seat before the driver stepped on the gas pedal, closing the door quickly before it hit the white electric garage gate that was slowly opening.

It was midmorning by now and traffic was light. They drove on the inside road of Boca Grande, past the naval base and into the Avenida San Martin along the beaches of Cartagena. They rounded the old city which is surrounded by and ancient wall over 12 feet tall built by the Spanish to protect the city from attacking ships. They continued the shoreside road past Marbella to the end of the airport and turned into the first road that led to Million Air Cartagena, the small private plane terminal.

Rodrigo opened the door before Lucho could stop the SUV in front of the Bombardier Challenger 300 jet and stepped out. Waving a hand at his pilot Sableta, he climbed the steps into the cool cabin of the jet. A girl with short black hair wearing a grey apron over her blue uniform greeted Rodrigo and asked him if he wanted something to drink before departure. Rodrigo waved to the girl shaking his head and sat on one of the leather seats with the most leg room. Jairo walked behind him and took a seat in the bulkhead row. They were up in the air within 15 minutes.

CHAPTER 11

Mermaids were swimming around him. He could hear them giggling and laughing, but wait, sound underwater does not travel like this. He was waking up; Susana and Victoria were the ones giggling and laughing about something Ray had said. Ice cubes from a cooler, the smell of home-made food, it was all coming together.

Chris sat on the hammock for a minute getting his bearings back when Victoria approached him with a glass and said: "Salud! The captain is cooking lasagna for us. It will be ready in about twenty minutes. Thank you again Chris."

"You're very welcome, Victoria. You look rested and refreshed" said Chris as he stood from the hammock and stretched.

The sun was starting to hide behind La Borracha island. It was going to be another beautiful and clear evening. A light breeze had the bow of the boat pointing at the beach and the view from the stern was out of a postcard. Some Reggae tunes were coming out of speakers on the boat but not too loud. Chris felt relaxed and was very glad the girls were not hurt or traumatized. They were strong girls but still It had been a close call. He believed that if they had been there an hour or two later, they would have probably been telling a different story. But what was it about trouble always finding them, he kept wondering. He took a sip from the glass and said: "Um! Cuba Libre! What kind of rum is this?"

Cacique! Ray replied with a smile on his face and raised his glass towards Chris.

Excelente! "Chris said taking another sip and walking towards a bench where his ditch bag was. He grabbed his phone and saw that he had two missed calls: One call from Rick and another one from General Pineda. He took the phone and his drink and walked aft to call Rick.

"Rick! Chris Dunn."

"Secured?" Rick replied from the other end.

"Encrypted" replied Chris.

"We heard some fireworks earlier, was it you?" Rick asked.

"Maybe yes, maybe no. It depends on who's asking" Chris replied.

"Well, rumors are one of their speedboats crashed on the side of the cargo ship and it's still burning by its side. We hear that Mr. Escalante is not a happy man these days and nobody seem to know how it happened. Watch your six Chris. We'll be close by but cannot make a move into Venezuelan waters. This guy has all kinds of government and military crooks in his pocket."

"Thank you for your support" Chris replied with some sarcasm in his tone.

"We know you'll keep squeezing until the rats come out Chris" Rick said and the call ended.

Chris never trusted a single source of intelligence, so his next call was to General Pineda in Caracas.

"General, Chris Dunn!" he spoke after the general answered the call.

"Chris, I've been trying to reach you about your inquiry from yesterday's call. I can confirm that yes, there is some activity by a cartel out of Cartagena, Colombia. The head is a dangerous man by the name of Rodrigo Escalante. He has connections in Mexico, Panama and Venezuela. Rumors has it that he feeds small cargo ship bound for Mexico and Panama from the eastern coast of Venezuela. Mules run the drugs northeast and northwest from Mexico and into the Caribbean, and South Pacific from the Panama Canal zone. Do be careful because he has the government here in his pocket with incentives and bonuses."

"This is very helpful as always general. Thank you very much" Chris said.

"Keep your head on a swivel Chris. This guy is well connected to the government here!" General Pineda told Chris.

"General, can I ask you a favor?" asked Chris.

"You can ask all you want" replied the general.

"Could you send me a care package? We'll be anchored at Las Isletas tomorrow" said Chris.

"You'll have it there by noon Chris" said the general before they said their goodbyes and ended the call.

General Pineda saw Chris as a son that he never had. Chris' father and a younger General Pineda had become good friends while they were both stationed in Caracas. They both knew that their conversations always ended up with each other exchanging intel information during the cold war days. On Saturdays, the general would always ask Chris to go for hikes with him around the hills of the military fort in Caracas. Chris always looked forward to running and hiking with him. Later the General married and had two daughters who each had a daughter each. So, the general treated and supported Chris like his own son.

Chris walked back and sat at the table with Ray, Susana, Victoria and Captain Giovanni. The captain was cutting into a deep dish of lasagna and serving it on plates for everyone. The mood was light with conversation, laughs and the music still going. Eduardo was filling and replacing air tanks on the racks for the dives of the next day. You could hear the air compressor running. They ate salad and bread followed with chocolate ice cream sandwiches.

"Captain Giovanni stood up and said: "Excuse me for a few minutes." And he climbed up the bridge.

Less than five minutes he called Chris and asked him to come up to the bridge.

"We may have company approaching" said Giovanni pointing on the screen at a yellow arrow generated by the AIS signal on the Donzy speedboat.

"How far out are they?" Chris asked the captain.

"They are about 15 miles out, but they will need to turn between the islands before they get here. My best guess is that they'll be here in about 20 to 25 minutes."

"Captain, we're about to make a disappearance act. We'll hide inside the cave around the point, and you tell them that we drove back to Caracas this morning. Don't let them board the boat. Keep as many lights out as you can, dark is good. I don't want to get into a fight with these guys having so much collateral around. Wish us luck" said Chris.

"You got it Chris! If my running lights are on, that's your all-clear signal" replied Giovanni.

"That's very smart Captain!" said Chris.

"I'm not any smarter than the average guy out there Chris, I'm just older than the average guy" Giovanni replied with a crooked smile on his face.

Chris climbed down the steps from the bridge and addressed Ray and the two girls: "Gang, we should go for a fun night dive. It's a beautiful evening."

The girls looked at each other, Ray raised an eyebrow, and the girls almost simultaneously answered: "We are beat, we'll sit this one out".

"Well, here is the thing, we are about to have bad company" Chris said with a smirk.

Before Chris could finish his sentence, everyone got up and started running around to get ready for the night dive.

Chris said out loud: "Try to put all your belongings below so that they cannot be seen from other boats, don't forget the cameras and the dive bags. We need to show them a clear deck."

Susana had almost done all her SCUBA gear and was checking the airflow in the hoses when she asked Ray: "Are we taking the tender?" Ray looked at Chris with both hands open with palms in the air.

Chris responded: "The tender stays tied to the boat. We're swimming on the surface until we get to that point. There we'll submerge and just follow my lead. It won't be a deep dive. It will be fun. Let's hit the water."

With Eduardo helping the girls enter the water and Chris and Ray following, it was not long before they were swimming on the surface towards the tip of Chimana Grande. When Chris could hear the engines of a boat slowing down, he signaled to the group to dive. They switched from their snorkels to their dive regulator and descended about thirty feet with their lights on. Once they gathered on the sandy bottom Chris signaled them to follow him. They swam very close to the cliff of the island until they found the opening Chris was looking for. One by one they went through the opening of the cave. Chris turned his dive light off and waited to go last.

Once inside the cave Chris signaled the three divers to turn their dive lights off. It became dark, but there was still enough light emanating from the chemicals inside the green glow sticks that the girls still had attached to their SCUBA tanks the night before. Under the reflection of the green glow, Chris signaled the divers to swim to the surface. Susana and Victoria looked at each other as Ray started swimming towards the surface. The girls followed

Ray until they were floating inside the cave filled with air inside. Chris surfaced last, lower his mask under his chin and said: "It's okay, you can breathe the air inside here." Ray was already taking his regulator mouthpiece out of his mouth. The girls were a bit more skeptical and slower about removing their regulators and taking that first gulp of air.

The air was musty and salty inside the cave. The walls inside the cave had fossils imbedded in the rock and the dome was about twelve feet high. On the far side, there was a ledge with small rocks and pebbles against the wall.

Chris carefully swam towards the end of the cave. He took off his dive gear, climbed on the ledge, turned around and sat on the rock. "Take the load off" he said with a smile. His mask under his chin, his fins still on and inside the water. The rest of the group joined him one by one. By now their eyes had adjusted to the poor light of the glowing sticks and they could observe their surroundings.

Looking around the inside of the cave, Ray asked the group: "Has any of you heard the story of a diver that was stuck inside a river cave much smaller than this one for three days?"

"No!" said Susana,

"When was this? asked Victoria.

"Was it around here?" asked Susana.

Chris smiled because he was aware of the story since his friend had been part of the rescue team that found the diver. It brought him very happy memories since they knew then that they were going to recover a body, not a diver alive.

"No" replied Ray as he continued telling the story.

"It all happened outside not far from Caracas over ten years ago in Riito de Acarite. This diver by the name of Gustavo… I can't recall his last name. It's been a while. Anyway, he and his buddy decide to go cave diving one day and Gustavo's girlfriend tags along as their safety person outside of the water. They had some thick lines, but nothing professional. I even remember hearing that they were diving with floating nylon lines. They started their dive according to Gustavo and it got cloudy and silty very quickly, because they were kicking the dirt behind them. At some point, the two divers got separated under zero visibility. Safety lines get dropped under panic; turns were made going in but were hard to determine those same turns going back. Gustavo's dive buddy miraculously made it out with the safety line. When he surfaced, he looked around and shouted to Gustavo's girlfriend: "Is Gustavo out here?" Gustavo's girlfriend stood up from her picnic blanket where she was getting lunch ready for the guys after their dive. She looked around, turned her head left to right and walked to the edge of the cold water.

Under the green glow, both Susana and Veronica kept staring at Ray wide eyed when Ray stopped to catch his breath. Ray smiled; he was enjoying the telling of the story inside a similar environment with very little light. Susana and Victoria looked like little kids listening to a scary story around a campfire at night.

Gustavo's dive buddy and girlfriend waited around 20 minutes. His dive buddy attempted to go back but the zero visibility and the cold-water temperature were too much for his anxiety and expertise. He started pulling on the safety lines, but nothing was at the end. Now, over thirty minutes have gone by, and Gustavo's dive buddy starts to worry about the air in the dive tank and air consumption. A full hour goes by since Gustavo' buddy surfaced.

Gustavo was working in a diving shop in Caracas at the time. His girlfriend contacted his boss, an expat from the U.S. who knew a group of cave and rescue divers from central Florida. Central Florida is well known for cave diving, and for cave diving fatalities too. Many of the dangerous caves have metal bars so as not to allow divers to continue inside. In some of the cave entrances there are signs with the number of cave divers' casualties.

Arrangements were made to have the rescue cave divers picked up in a private airplane of a family member of the diving shop owner. The plan was to fly them to a small airport outside of Caracas. By the time they picked up the cave rescue divers, with all their gear over a day and a half had gone by. Fog moves into the area, and they can't land a chopper nearby. So now they must make the trip in a Jeep and cross a mountain to get there.

Almost three days after Gustavo and his buddy had started their dive, the cave rescue divers entered the water with spools of lines in their reels, multiple air tanks and lights. Before they entered the water, they knew they were on a body recovery dive, not a rescue dive. Gustavo's girlfriend and his buddy never left the diving site in all three days.

Twenty minutes into the cave rescue recovery dive, one of the rescue divers surfaced with Gustavo breathing out of one of the separate alternate air sources he carried.

Everyone on shore was silent for what felt like a very long minute and then all the celebratory shouts came out while the second cave rescue diver was surfacing the water.

Gustavo tells that when he was running out of air, he had found an air pocket with a very small step on it that he could climb into. The area was not much bigger than a large moving cardboard box. He ditched his gear and climbed on the ledge, of course much smaller than this one. He says that after a day he had to get rid of his watch so that he couldn't tell the time anymore. After two days he got rid of the knife he carried in the inside of his leg for fear of killing himself before he died. After almost three days he was reborn when he saw one of the cave rescue divers surfaced inside the small air pocket.

"We have been looking for you, but never expected to find you alive" the cave rescue diver told Gustavo as they were getting ready to get out of the small air pocket. Gustavo was never the same after that incident inside that cave, but he was very thankful to both cave rescue divers for flying out there and finding him.

"Is that a true story?" Susana asked, turning her head to look at both Chris and Ray for an answer.

"Well Susana", Ray said, "let's say that nowadays it is a semi-true story, since some of it is true and the other, I don't remember because it happened a long time ago. I believe there was some writing or documentary about it. I don't think it reached Hollywood, but it's out there. I am sure if you search for it, you'll find it. Also, Gustavo is still around. Last time I ran into him was at a DEMA Conference in Orlando. DEMA is the Diving Equipment &

Marketing Association. They have an annual conference, and we always run into people we know. I remember he was working for one of the institutes in the Florida Keys. We also ran into the cave rescue divers that same year at the conference."

"Why would they make a dive inside those caves without experience and the right gear for it? asked Susana.

"Well, it's like people who drive on the highway in a rainstorm" explained Ray. Suddenly, when it starts pouring rain they step on the brakes in the middle of the highway and the rest of the traffic is moving at sixty or seventy miles an hour. If you don't or can't drive in the rain, you should not be out driving, much less on a highway."

"You can't just go on an impulse and try to dive in a different environment with the same gear and experience you've had. It requires additional training, gear and a state of mind to get out of trouble down there. You must consider visibility, cold water, restricted spaces, redundancy in your gear and most important a plan for the worst-case scenarios."

Both girls nodded in agreement trying to imagine the scenario of the incident that Ray had just told them about.

"I'm going outside the cave and to the surface to see if we have an all-clear sign from Captain Giovanni" Chris said.

Chris got a nod from all three, placed his mask on his face and slid into his SCUBA rig buckling it as he swam down and out of the cave. He surfaced slowly without a light on and with his back against the cliff of the island, and in the background, he could hear the small boat engines moving away from them. He turned sideways to look for the Old Chris Craft and a second later, the red and green running lights came on each side of Giovanni's boat. Chris floated for a few more minutes to make sure the running lights didn't go off and that the sound of the boat running didn't return.

Diving back down and up inside the cave, he surfaced and said: "I don't think we are in the clear, but it's safe to swim back to the boat."

Susana asked what he meant by saying we were not in the clear.

"It seems that trouble has a way of finding us Susana" Chris said. "These guys are not going to give up this easy. They will come back for their revenge at us burning their deposit of drugs. Like I said, It's not over yet."

"I don't believe you guys go around looking for trouble. You're just those guys we are all glad are there for us when trouble shows up its ugly face. We cannot thank you enough for what you did. Who knows where we could have ended up. I don't even want to think about it. Thank you again!" said Susana almost with tears.

"Okay," Chris said. "Let's head back to the boat, but surface slowly just in case they turned around for a second look. Keep your dive lights off. Your eyes should be well adjusted by now and Captain Giovanni has the running lights of the boat on. Just swim towards the green and red lights."

Susana and Victoria went first down and out of the cave. Chris and Ray followed the dimmed green lights on the tanks. They surfaced slowly and quietly and started swimming towards the old Chris Craft. Once they reached the swim platform, they started handing Eduardo their dive gear and climbed out.

Once on the deck, they started disassembling their gear and rinsing it with freshwater. They got out of their wetsuits, rinsed them and took freshwater showers.

Captain Giovanni came down from the bridge and said: "It seems they headed back towards Santa Fe. What would you like to do?"

"We need a safe and quite place to regroup Captain" Chris said. "Are you okay with running at night to Las Isletas? It's about a twenty-mile run west by southwest from here. We could run dark for a while and that would take some of the load from you."

"Eduardo let's get the tender ready for tow. Secure the decks and let's get ready to weigh anchor. We are running dark" Captain Giovanni said.

Eduardo and the dive team all got to work securing diving gear, tanks, bags, cameras until they heard chain being pulled into the boat by the windlass.

CHAPTER 12

The Bombardier Challenger 300 landed on a small private airstrip after a low altitude approach. The landing strip was part of a farm that Escalante had acquired from a corrupt Venezuelan army colonel. The landing strip had been cut into the mountain a long time ago and made pilots sweat every time they had to land and take off because of the cliffs surrounding the airstrip.

Embedded into the mountain was a villa with gardens and built roads bordering the mountain to the airstrip and into Santa Fe. The lush green mountain vegetation reminded Rodrigo of the mountains around Medellin.

Rodrigo looked out of the window and felt like he could almost touch the red clay on the side of the mountain when they were landing. As soon as the plane slowed down, even before it came to a stop, he was already up straightening his shirt and putting his coat jacket back on. By the time the young flight attendant unstrapped from her seat and lowered the door, Escalante was right behind her impatiently waiting to step down from the plane.

Another black Nissan Armada was parked with its rear passenger door open and his driver and Wilfredo standing by it. Wilfredo extended his hand, but Escalante kept walking and climbed inside the Nissan SUV. The driver closed the door and ran around to climb into the driver seat, while Wilfredo got into the front passenger seat.

"Qué pasa?" Escalante almost shouted at Wilfredo.

"Jefe, unos gringos." Wilfredo started to respond but was interrupted by Escalante.

"Cómo que unos Gringos?" shouted Escalante.

"Si, unos gringos assaulted me on the Cigarette boat and drove me up to the caves" Wilfredo said almost in a whisper." They tied us up, burnt the deposit and took the old Land Rover."

"How did they know we were using the caves as a deposit?" Escalante asked.

"We don't know" replied Wilfredo lowering his head and thinking about the girls they had picked up.

"Dale! Dale! Baja a Santa Fe!" Escalante ordered the driver.

The driver accelerated and started negotiating the curves on the narrow mountain dirt road taking them towards the main and wider road that led to Santa Fe.

"Jefe, we should drive by the cove and see if the boats are still there. I didn't have time or means to drive down there and check on them," said Wilfredo

Escalante didn't say another word until they were driving into the parking area above the cliff.

After getting out of the Nissan Wilfredo and Escalante looked down towards the cove and noticed the Cigarette speedboat missing.

"Vamos!" Escalante ordered Wilfredo as he started stepping down towards the beach. He then turned and shouted up the hill to Jairo to stay there and to try to find out what was going on.

Wilfredo followed.

They climbed on the yellow and white Donzi. Escalante sat on the side passenger seat while Wilfredo started the boat, pulled the anchor and stowed it away in the anchor locker. He then backed out of the cove and brought the fast boat up on a plane.

"Head out to the ship" he ordered Wilfredo.

They headed northwest out to sea.

After three miles they saw their Cigarette speedboat and it appeared to be just floating out there. Wilfredo pushed the throttle down to gain more speed. As they got closer, they noticed that the speedboat was getting up on a plane with a north heading. By the sound and looks of it, it was running full throttle out to sea.

Wilfredo made the slight turn towards the north in pursuit of the Cigarette boat, but he knew there was no way he could catch up with it, not even if the Cigarette speedboat was going at half throttle.

Escalante turned to look at Wilfredo and he put his hands palms up like asking: what do you want me to do?

Escalante lowered himself into the passenger side seat fuming in frustration.

After six more miles of running after the speedboat, they heard and saw the explosion only three miles from them.

By the time they approached the ship, the Cigarette speedboat was burning with a 15 feet flame over it. The crew of the ship was spraying saltwater from the pumps into it and the captain was trying to maneuver the ship away from the fire.

"Go around!" Escalante shouted at Wilfredo over all the noise and heat from the flames.

Wilfredo maneuvered the Donzi around the ship trying to stay away from the ship's stern and its propellers. He brought the yellow and white boat along the port side of the ship but had to wait for a crew member to catch a line and tie it to a large cleat.

Escalante couldn't wait any longer and he jumped over to the lowered boarding ladder hanging from the ship's port side. He climbed up and found his way to the bridge.

"What's going on?" he shouted at the captain over all the commotion.

"We don't know. That boat came directly towards us at high speed. We don't even know if there's someone on board. We were expecting another shipment, not a kamikaze," the captain explained between shouts at his crew with instructions. "We're trying to move the ship away from the boat so that we don't catch on fire."

"How much is on board?" asked Escalante.

"The next load was going to make a thousand kilos" replied the captain of the ship.

"Get out of here and do try to save it! Go!" shouted Escalante over all the noise.

The captain gave the orders to secure the decks and to turn the boat on a 318 heading at 10 knots.

Escalante ran to the port side and climbed back down the boarding ladder shouting at the ship crew member who was trying to untie it.. He kept thinking about what earful he was going to get from La Jefa.

"Let's go!" Escalante shouted at Wilfredo over the sound of the ship's engines and propellers.

The ship started to drag the boat on its port side until the ship's crew member dropped the bowline on the small boat. Wilfredo steered away from the ship trying to avoid the wake it was about to throw at them.

"Let's find those gringos!" shouted Escalante

Wilfredo turned southeast towards Chimana Grande with the sun going down in front of them. It was hard for him to navigate with the sun glimmering on the water right in front of him at least until the sun went behind some of the islands and the mainland. They steered past Cachicamo and El Faro, and south of Chimana Grande until they spotted the old Chris Craft. It was getting dark now.

Escalante and Wilfredo scouted the waters between the Chimanas slowing down near the starboard side of the old Chris Craft.

Captain Giovanni shouted at them from above on the side of the bridge: "Don't scratch my hull with that new boat." A big smile on his face. "How can I help you?"

"Los gringos?" shouted Escalante.

"Se fueron a Caracas" shouted the captain pointing towards the mainland.

Escalante and Wilfredo stayed there floating for a while looking at the deck of the old Chris Craft in the dark. Eduardo laying on one of the hammocks with his legs and arms hanging outside of it as if sleeping.

Captain Giovanni didn't offer to catch a line or throw them a line to tie up. After five minutes they navigated around the boat and headed back towards what Captain Giovanni would later confirm was Santa Fe. Also, the fact that the Guarda Costa cutter was cruising around the area made their departure premature.

Escalante's phone vibrated in his pocket. He answered it. He had to shout over the noise of the wind and the boat engines.

"Rodrigo, what's this I hear about my shipment being short this time?" the voice on the phone said.

LAS ISLETAS

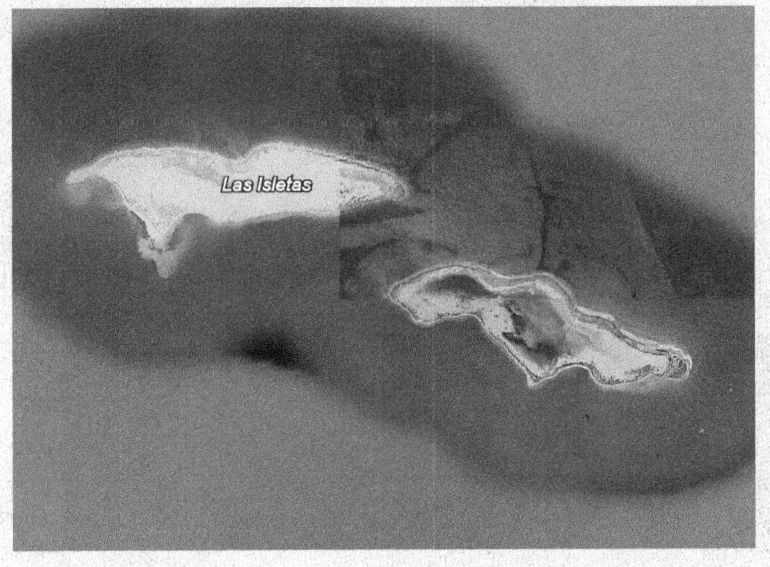

CHAPTER 13

Las Isletas lies fifteen miles southwest of La Borracha. These two flat islands are completely different from their sister islands to the east. They are much closer to the mainland, only three miles, and don't have the rocky cliffs or caves that the other islands have. The beaches around these flat islands are sandier and flatter, less rocky bottom, and more sand. They are almost like large sandbars.

They made the run in under two hours at a slow ten knots towing the tender behind. There is nothing like running at night in the dark on a boat, sailing or powerboating. There is something about the lack of light, the depth perception, even the sounds are different when running at night. More stars than you can look at cover the skies.

It's almost like being in a different world when you run at night on a boat.

Chris had joined Captain Giovanni on the bridge since the rest of the diving party had gone to sleep or had fallen asleep inside the hammocks. They sat there in silence for a while enjoying the night run until Chris asked Captain Giovanni how long he had been running around in these waters.

"Over twenty-five years Chris! I used to run trips out to La Tortuga, La Orchila and Los Roques out of Higuerote. I had higher paying customers, but also more expenses. One day a uniformed Guardia Nacional was standing on the dock as we were about to return from Los Roques. He approached the boat and asked if he could get a ride on the boat to Higuerote. Nice Captain Mango here, told the Guardia to jump on. He helped with the lines and was very happy to catch a ride back home for his weekend leave. Word got out and later it felt like I was giving these guides free rides to and from those islands for nothing in exchange. I felt like it was something I had to do to get better treatment docking in and out. The number of customers started to decrease, trips became further apart, but the boat docking, and maintenance continued and at higher prices. It was then that I decided to move the boat out here near the Mochima National Park and cater to divers and snorkelers. Of course, later came some good contracts like the ones I have with the Universities, private researchers, and underwater photographers."

"Of course, I would rather have you guys on board than the typical weekend diver coming from Caracas. You guys are low maintenance. I don't have to pamper you guys or be on top of your gear being ready. It gives me more time to cook for you guys, which I like very much second to my boat. It also gives Eduardo and me more time to work on the maintenance of the boat."

"Give me a second" Giovanni said and stood from his chair to change the heading to avoid a container ship going into the port of Puerto La Cruz.

"Do you get a lot of container ship traffic around here?" Chris asked pointing at the container ship.

"It gets worst in the months of October and November" Giovanni replied.

"Why is that? Chris asked.

"Well, you see, the ports customs are controlled by the same Guardia Nacional. They decide what comes in and out of the ports and with what urgency. If you're importing goods, parts, supplies, and you want your container to move through customs quicker, you must show your generosity to them. In the summer months these higher corrupt officials go on a shopping spree out of the country and bring in containers full of toys, clothing, electronics, sporting goods, to be sold here so that they can make extra monies for their holiday parties and year-end vacations. You can tell when the containers start coming in because the street vendors start appearing like ants. Of course, these containers have a free and agile passage through customs because the contents belong to their bosses."

"If your containers are marked for inspection, they are put aside and can sit at the port for a long time, or until the content starts to rot. This is also known as a Japanese inspection around the ports of the world. I guess it happens in other places, but here it's just easier for the common guy with two eyes to see and figure out, since it happens right in front of you. Or you can just read the news. Yesterday the plane of our president was seized at a private hangar on an airport in the Dominican Republic. The plane, a Dassault Falcon 900EX, they said it was seized because of illegalities, in violation of US sanctions with Venezuela and other criminal matters, but they haven't published the details. Chris, it's corruption and criminals from the top down" commented captain Giovanni.

"I see!" was all that Chris could say about that, trying to put some logic into it.

A few minutes passed and Chris asked the captain: "Giovanni, why do they call you Captain Mango? I haven't figured out if it's an insulting nickname for you or if you like it. You seemed to respond well to the nickname while we were loading at the dock."

The captain laughed: "I own five acres and a home between Higuerote and Rio Chico with very rich soil. We have all kinds of fruit trees that grow like weed all year round. All the mangos, limes, oranges, and papayas on the boat come from there. I always carry buckets of mangoes with me to the boat and always end up handing them out at the dock to other people."

Captain Giovanni started to ease on the throttles as the boat approached the Isletas islands. He steered the boat between the two islands and asked Eduardo to tend the windlass on the bow. The anchor chain started to drop down from the windlass once the captain had turned the boat into Playa Isleta on the western side of the island. That is my best guess as to why they call me Captain Mango. The nickname got stuck on me.

"Captain Mango!" Chris said slowly and smiling.

"How about you? You and Ray are not the typical marine biologists or oceanographers" asked the captain, turning to face Chris.

"We all have our dark sides captain. We all do" and Chris left it at that.

Captain Giovanni turned back to the chart plotter and radar displays.

"Captain, I did notice when we landed at the airport, many workers with Cuban accent? Has Venezuela had such a representative Cuban migration lately?" Chris asked.

"Oh! Yes," replied captain Giovanni. "We have had a lot of people migrate from Cuba lately, thanks to the last two presidents that called themselves democrats. You see, this country has slowly turned into another Cuba. The government here ships oil and gas to Cuba in exchange for what Cuba can supply, and we're not getting the star baseball players. High 'government officials cannot trust anyone here to protect them, so they recruit and bring their own security from Cuba. Also, the shortage of human resources has been backfilled with Cubans, doctors, nurses, dentists. That's why you'll hear people with Cuban accent like in Miami. So, the short answer to your question is: Yes."

When captain Giovanni turned the engines off and the humming sound of the generator was the only noise, Chris found an empty hammock and fell asleep immediately under a light breeze and comfortable temperatures.

The next morning everyone on board was busy before breakfast collecting gear and organizing bags. Captain Giovanni was cooking omelets and serving them inside toasted baguettes. We all sat down around the table with coffee and papaya juice to wash the omelet sandwiches. In between bites and sips of the sweet papaya juice we discussed the day's plans.

Las Isletas is not a place where you would go SCUBA diving since most of the islands are surrounded by sandy bottoms. It's a great place to anchor and jump in the water. It was squaring up to be a more relaxed day.

After breakfast they cleaned up, everyone started jumping off the stern deck into the water and swimming to the beach. Chris was the last one in the water and Eduardo handed him a sealed plastic container to take to the beach.

The beach around the island belonged at the edge of a five-star resort. The white sand and the crystalline water had the group enjoying themselves for a break. Around noon Ray walked back into the water where the group was engaged in small talk. He was carrying the plastic container that Eduardo had sent with Chris. He passed it around and everyone started to savor slices of very sweet mango. A noise from far away slowed down the conversations and everyone became silent. They turned to see a small peñero or panga painted with blue, red and yellow stripes coming towards them. Ray asked no one in particular: 'Are we expecting company?"

"It must be our care package from General Pineda," Chris replied.

Two young men approached in the peñero towards the beach where they were standing. They beached the peñero and lifted the outboard so that it wouldn't get buried in the sand. One of the young men jumped in the water, turned around and grabbed a black cooler bag from inside the peñero. He started walking towards Chris extending his arms with the bag and spoke: "Delivery from El General, Mister Chris."

Chris grabbed the bag not expecting its weight, also not knowing how the young man new who he was and said: "Gracias!"

The young man turned around, walked back to the peñero and pushed it back into deeper water. He climbed back on it. Once in deeper water, the other young man at the tiller lowered and started the small outboard. Once the outboard was running, they backed out and left.

Chris took the bag to the beach, placed it on the sand covering it with a towel and walked back to the water to join the others in the water.

In the early afternoon they started swimming back to the boat and got out of the water. Chris was the last one and approaching the boat he handed the heavy black bag to Ray. When Chris climbed onto the boat, he opened the bag while Ray was looking over his shoulders.

"It's like Christmas around here" said Ray admiring all the new toys well cushioned and wrapped inside the bag.

Chris looked around to make sure no one was looking and started to examine the contents of the bag. The care package from the general included a couple of semi-automatic 9 millimeters Glock 19 and two Glock 26 subcompact bored with the same caliber. They were already loaded with 15 round magazines and additional magazines for them. A set of binoculars and set of night vision gear still packed inside their cases. In addition, there were two combat tactical knives, and two automatic switchblade knives. At the bottom of the bag lay a bunch of heavy-duty cable ties and additional boxes of ammunition. A note that Chris had been holding all along laid on top of everything. Chris put all the contents back in the bag and read the note.

"I can only hope this care package will help the cause. Please destroy after use."

Chris handed Ray the note. Ray read it and then made confetti out of it. Chris stowed the bag below with his belongings.

Captain Giovanni had baked Arepas for lunch and they stuffed them with chicken salad. Ray asked the captain if he had more papaya juice, and he walked back with a whole pitcher of the sweet juice, and they all laughed.

"I just can't have enough of this juice captain!" said Ray still laughing.

They all helped to pick up after lunch and the girls were starting to get comfortable in the hammocks with a light breeze from the east.

Ray looked at them and then at Chris and said: "I don't want to rain on your beach day, but we have to log at least six more dives before the end of the week."

"Oh! Not now!" Susana said.

Victoria made a sad face.

Chris nodded and with a smile: "You're right. We need to get back to work before the captain makes us fat, stuffs a mango in our mouths and broils us for dinner."

"I heard that!" captain Giovanni shouted from above. "It's not a bad idea."

Ray was now looking at a waterproof chart of the park and said: "If we dive Picuda Grande and Picuda Chica, I believe it would give us a good range and distances between samples and transects."

"How far are we from Picuda Chica?" Chris asked Ray.

"Thirty miles to Picuda Chica and thirty-four miles to Picuda Grande from here" Ray responded after a few seconds while measuring the distances on the chart.

"Let's plan on making two dives around Picuda Chica tomorrow and one shallow night dive" Chris proposed.

They all agreed on the plan and suddenly it was very quiet except for the light breeze and the humming of the generator on the boat. Each one of them thinking about what they had to accomplish the next day.

Chris laid inside the hammock for a while and couldn't fall asleep. He was not used to taking naps in the afternoons. He got out of the hammock and climbed to the bridge to find captain Giovanni.

Captain Giovanni was looking at the chart plotter and reviewing waypoints and routes. He looked up and said to Chris: "There's some rain coming our way, but it will probably not hang around for long, maybe for less than an hour."

"What are your thoughts about heading east towards Picuda Chica for an early morning, afternoon and night dives?" Chris asked the captain.

"It's up to you guys. Do you think the coast is clear of those smugglers?" replied captain Giovanni.

"We'll be fine captain. They think we left to the safety of the city" said Chris. "Plus, now we have acquired some new toys to fight back just in case they return."

The captain nodded and said: "Very well! We have a plan. Picuda Chica it is."

After a moment of thought, the captain continued: "We need to make a stop and reprovision. I didn't plan for the additional two days out here. We will not have enough gasoline for the generator and the air compressor for three more days. We could also use some fresh bread, milk, fruit and vegetables. I can call ahead and have my provisioning guys bring it to the boat at the dock to save time."

"Would you meet them at Marina Inbuca in El Morro or at America Vespucio marina by Pueblo Viejo?" Chris asked.

"America Vespucio will be our best choice and better-quality fuel. Also, if you or the girls need anything else, it will be closer there" replied the captain.

"More limes would be great. When do you want to be on our way?" Chris asked.

"Let's plan to be underway in an hour. That will give us enough time to get there with some daylight" said the captain.

"Excelente!" said Chris.

The rain started to make some noise against the windshield of the bridge. Chris went below to let the crew know that they were moving within an hour. The girls were getting up from their hammocks and stretching. Ray had wrapped himself around his hammock and was still napping with his head hanging to a side. The spray of the rain woke him up and he gave us a look like it was our fault he was getting wet.

"We are weighing anchor within an hour. The captain wants to reprovision and he's calling ahead, so if you want or need anything, let him know so that he can call it in. We're fueling up and picking up the provisions at Americo Vespucio marina. We should be clearing the jetties inside the marina in two hours."

Ray looked around and then asked with the palms of his hands facing up: "Who's this Americo Vespucio guy? And why did he get a marina name after him?"

Victoria put her hands on her hips, looked at Ray and said: "I cannot believe that you don't know who Americo Vespucio is Ray, you of all people?"

Ray looked at Susana and Chris for a way out but couldn't find one and said: "I guess I'm the only one who doesn't know about this guy and you're about to lecture me, right?"

"He was an Italian explorer and navigator from Florence way back in the fifteen hundreds. He was the guy responsible for naming the New World on charts as America. There was a lot of controversies about it, but at the end he was credited for it" Victoria explained.

"Oh! Oh! That guy!" Ray said. "But wasn't his name Amerigo Vespucci? Oh! I get it now! Amerigo, Americo and Vespucci, Vespucio. Got it!"

They all laughed at the same time until the captain started the diesel engines and Eduardo started to bring the chain from the anchor onto the boat with the windlass. A few minutes later they were on a northwest heading towards El Morro.

CHAPTER 14

"What do you mean by two gringos, marica?"

Cecilia Machado was not having a good day. A few minutes earlier one of her goons aboard the cargo ship Tzini alerted her that their shipment was short by a hundred kilos. He also mentioned the incident with the speedboat and the explosion on the side of the ship

"Jefa, we haven't found them yet, but they burnt our next ship load as well. A total of one thousand and one hundred kilos." Rodrigo Escalante closed his eyes and shouted into his phone over the noise of the engines, and the wind flowing over the windshield of the speedboat. He knew what was coming.

"Mira marica, you find those gringos and bring them to me, entiendes? Bring me those fucking gringos" Cecilia yelled at him.

"Si Jefa! Si!" It was all he could answer before the line went dead.

Rodrigo threw his phone against the deck of the boat and shouted: "Carajo! I hate that lesbian witch."

Wilfredo sank deeper into the bucket seat of the boat.

Cecilia Machado, also known as The Witch of the Mountain, was the controlling individual of a drug cartel behind many operations. Rumors say that she killed her husband just to take over the cartel. Born in Cali, Colombia, Cecilia was never in one place for a very long time. She owned houses, apartments, villas, some even say she owned a small unknown island in the Caribbean. She jumped from place to place with an entourage of dangerous killers. Some of the places known by the DEA included Cartagena, Cali, Medellin, San Andres, Panama, Miami and even Caracas and New York city.

Machado's cartel was responsible for most of the drug traffic into the Caribbean, Central and North America. Her signature was to play the magician hands of allowing capture to a small shipment, while the larger shipment was in transit. She had been known to use small submarines, planes, boats and trucks to move drugs across countries and into demanding markets. She had mobile labs, and plantations in different areas and countries. The DEA had been trying to infiltrate her operations but ended up with a small group of smugglers with a few kilos of illegal substances. Interpol had been also on a trail of human traffic pointing at Cecilia Machado as the head of it and user of the products herself.

Rodrigo hated Cecilia for her attitude towards him and her insults. He never did a job right or handled his people in the proper manner according to Machado. It was always not enough or too much. He worked too hard, or he didn't work enough. He had too much overhead, or not enough resources. It was always negative feedback from her. But Rodrigo always talked himself out of the hate for her because it was all about money. Money, he needed to maintain his vices and luxurious lifestyle, his plane, his apartments, his cars, his grunts, his security.

Wilfredo slowed down the Donzi speedboat as they approached the cove inside Bahia Los Coquitos. Waiting for them up on the hill were Jairo, Rodrigo's grunt and the driver. Rodrigo jumped from the boat before Wilfredo had a chance to turn the engines off and drop the anchor next to the peñeros already anchored there. He followed Rodrigo up the steps off the cliff. Rodrigo stopped in front of Jairo and said: "Find me those gringos!" He climbed inside the black Nissan Armada SUV and told the driver: "Take me to the villa," and they were gone. Wilfredo and Jairo stood there looking at each other not knowing how to proceed.

Jairo told Wilfredo to open the doors of the old Land Cruiser. Wilfredo with his hands opened said:" I don't have the keys. The gringos took them. I don't know where they left them." They checked all doors and finally Jairo grabbed a rock from the edge of the cliff and busted the driver's window of the Land Cruiser. He opened the door, unfolded a pocketknife and leaned under the steering column to cut some of the cables to the ignition switch.

When Jairo tried to start the Land Cruiser, the old rustic vehicle jumped and almost went over the cliff. The frame of the door hit Jairo on the side and slammed him onto the ground. He stood up, looked at Wilfredo and slammed the door so hard it almost came off its hinges. He then shouted at Wilfredo: "You drive!"

Wilfredo, still in shock, and holding his laughter, climbed into the driver seat with all the shattered glass, placed the shifter into neutral and shorted the ignition cables. The Old Land Cruiser started. He turned towards Jairo as he climbed into the passenger seat and sked him: "Where to?"

"I don't know" responded Jairo still in pain and holding his side. Let's go where that boat could have unloaded those gringos and the girls. Maybe the marinas. Go! Drive!"

Wilfredo turned the Land Cruiser towards the road: "I think it can only be three marinas where that boat would load and unload tourists. El Morro, Americo Vespucio and Marina Vieja."

"Don't think, just drive" Jairo told Wilfredo, still in pain. "Start with the closest one."

"Marina Vieja is the closest one" Wilfredo said as they headed west towards Puerto La Cruz.

They drove in silence thinking about the trouble these gringos had created for them. If heads had to roll it was going to be theirs, no question about that.

Once they were on Paseo Colon Avenue, they followed it past the ferry terminal and continued to the end of it where Marina Vieja was. They drove around the high and dry warehouses to the waterfront. They stopped at the Casa de Playa lounge for a beer in the late afternoon. When they walked out to the parking lot of the lounge in the early evening, they saw the old Chris Craft boat tied up on the seawall across the canal. They climbed inside Land Rover and drove to the water's edge to take a closer look. The Chris Craft was at the fuel dock, and they were loading boxes inside the boat. They could not see who was on the other side of the boat. Wilfredo backed the Land Rover and drove forward. We need to talk to the captain of that boat before it leaves the dock.

PICUDA CHICA

CHAPTER 15

The rainstorm was now behind them. It turned out to be a beautiful evening as they rounded El Morro and headed towards the breakwaters along Playa El Doral. Ray had some Supertramp music going on the boat's speakers.

"Can we order pizza for dinner?" Susana asked while looking at the outline of the beach.

They were all seating around the bridge enjoying the ride along the coast.

"Order pizza? On my boat? I'm insulted---" answered Captain Giovanni with a smile. "Okay, I'll allow it, but only because I will not have enough time to cook for you tonight. With the fueling, loading provisions, docking and departure, it's going to get late. Go ahead and order it now so you can pick them up when we dock the boat."

Susana's frown changed to a smile, and she went to search for the pizza place on her phone.

I would like to make this stop short in time so that we can get to Picuda Chica at a decent hour. If You and Ray can help Eduardo load the provisions and put them away, I'll do the fueling. Susana and Victoria can go after the pizzas." The captain said.

"Would you like anything in particular in your pizzas?" Susana asked.

"I'll eat anything on my pizza except onions."

"I'd like a veggie pizza" Ray said, and everyone turned to look at him. "What? Can't a man watch his figure? More limes would be great too." Everyone laughed.

Giovanni, Eduardo and Victoria all said they were fine with anything on their pizzas.

Two dock attendants were standing by to catch lines from Eduardo at the bow and Ray on the stern. Susana and Victoria stood by on the starboard side of the boat with spring lines ready to be handed down.

Captain Giovanni had called the marina ahead of time and he was instructed to dock on the seawall, since the boat was not staying for a long period of time. He had also contacted his provisioners and they were sitting on the bed of an old pickup truck waiting for them to dock.

Once Captain Giovanni was happy with the dock lines and fenders to protect the boat from being scratched by the seawall, everyone turned to their duties. Susana and Veronica jumped ship and started walking towards Johnny Pepper Pizzeria. The two guys on the old pick-up truck backed up closer to the boat and started handing boxes and bags to Chris and Ray. Eduardo stayed in the galley storing the provisions.

Captain Giovanni was having what seemed like an argument with the fuel dock attendants. Chris left Ray to finish loading the rest of the provisions and walked forward to where the captain was holding the fuel hose over the tank intake. "Is everything alright?" asked Chris to Captain Giovanni.

"It's always the same Chris! They are always complaining." Captain Giovanni said. Today they're complaining because we're late and they closed an hour ago. Tomorrow, they'll complain because they don't have enough business. Why can't people be flexible? How are we doing with the provisioning?"

"Ray is loading the last of it and Eduardo is storing in the galley" Chris replied.

"Do you mind handing me the bill from Juan?" Captain Giovanni asked, pointing at one of the guys closing the bed of the pickup truck.

"No problem!" Chris said.

Susana and Victoria were walking back to the boat with the pizzas and Victoria froze and stopped walking. Susana turned around and looked at her. "What's wrong?" Susana asked.

Victoria started walking again but at a faster pace. "I'll tell you in a minute" was all Victoria said.

As soon as Susana and Victoria were back on board the Chris Craft, they took the pizzas into the galley and went back out to the portside where Chris, Ray and Captain Giovanni were getting ready to cast off.

"Chris, I just saw one of the guys that kidnapped us two days ago. He was looking at the boat from the inside of that Land Cruiser across the canal." Victoria pointed across the canal. "I don't think they saw us because the boat was blocking their view, but they saw the boat. They were staring at it."

By the time they all turned around the Land Cruiser was moving towards Paseo Colon Av. Chris noticed that there were two guys inside but could not see their faces.

"Are we ready to cast off captain?" Chris asked Giovanni.

"We are ready! Eduardo, let's cast off, man the bow" Captain Giovanni shouted. "Ray, you're at the stern. Girls, the spring lines if you would. Everyone, wait for may signal. Let's go!"

They all scattered at a faster pace to their station. After casting off, captain Giovanni turned the boat around inside the basin and they headed back out passed the Guardia Costera station and the jetties.

Chris climbed to the bridge and turned aft trying to follow the Land Cruiser, but all the buildings and boats in the yard blocked his view of the roads. He started wondering if they had seen any of them from the other side of the channel. It was as if he immediately went on caution mode expecting the unexpected. Experience had trained Chris and Ray to always prepare for the worst. It was their universal mindset no matter where they were.

The run to Picuda Chica was uneventful. Susana and Victoria brought the pizzas and sodas up to the bridge, and they ate on their way. The evening breeze across the open doors of the bridge was cooling the air.

In between bites, Susana asked to no one in particular: "Do you think they saw us?"

"I couldn't tell. We were all on the other side of the boat. I couldn't see them, but they did see the boat" responded Ray.

They rounded the jetty protecting the basin from the waves and surge and turned to a northeast heading. A few minutes later, Victoria asked: "What are all those lights? Is that a building? It's moving!"

Giovanni turned and with a smile answered: "That's one of those ferries that goes from Puerto La Cruz to the island of Margarita. One must be careful at night around here. They don't see you unless you show up on their radar, and if they do see you, most likely it's going to be too late to avoid a collision. We'll slow down a bit and let them turn ahead of us. We'll follow them at a safe distance before we turn into Picuda Chica."

The Gran Cacique ferry turned heading northeast between the islands and the mainland, and they followed the wake about a mile behind. The radar was not showing boat traffic behind them. After about a seven-mile run behind the ferry, captain Giovanni slowly turned the boat north and steered clear of the two small islands of Quirica and Cachicamo. Like Picuda Chica, these small islands are just rock outcroppings coming out of the water and no bigger than five hundred yards wide. Picuda Chica has a small beach on its southwest side somewhat protected from the north and east winds. It is also surrounded by cliffs, caves and crevices.

Captain Giovanni slowed the boat down and asked Eduardo to get ready to drop the anchor. He lined up the boat parallel to the small beach and gave Eduardo the signal. After the boat had settled, they were looking at the small beach on the port side and the lights of the mainland 5 miles away on the starboard side of the boat.

It became very quiet when captain Giovanni turned the engines off. Only the humming noise of the generator in the background could be heard. They climbed down the steps to the stern deck and the view of the sky was hypnotizing. Stars were everywhere covering the night sky. The island seemed more like a black shadow in the darkness. The only light source was the small anchor light on top of the bridge.

"Look at the sky! This is amazing!" Victoria said looking up.

Ray was already stretching in one of the hammocks and shortly after the girls said their good nights and went below to sleep.

Chris sat inside another hammock across the deck, laid back and said to Ray: "I'm thinking about an early morning dive on the eastern side where the wall drops to over three hundred feet. We'll probably have some current that we can swim into in the shallows, drop down for the dive and then ride the current back to the boat."

"Early morning? Do you mean before breakfast? asked Ray.

"No, no, there is no rush, after breakfast" replied Chris.

"I didn't think so!" Ray came back.

"You know? Now that I have my work hat back on, I remember seeing a marine snake the night we went into the cave. When I went back out to check on Giovanni for the all-clear signal, I saw it swimming at the bottom, but I was more focused on our pursuers. I didn't know what to expect on the surface. I must remember to tell the girls when I have a chance.

Ray was already snoring, so Chris got out of the hammock and went below to grab a couple of light blankets. He threw one at Ray who turned to a side and continued snoring without missing a wink. Chris went back to his hammock, started feeling the slow motion of the boat rocking and in a few minutes was asleep.

The next morning brought a spectacular sunrise over the outline of the mountains in the mainland. Captain Giovanni had prepared empanadas for breakfast. He came out with a tray of the hot pastries and said: "The lighter colored ones have cheese inside. The darker reddish ones have Cazon. I hope you like them."

"What smells so good?" asked Susana walking up the companionway and joining the group around the table.

"Empanadas de Cazon y de queso" said Victoria.

"Remind me again, what is Cazon?" asked Ray.

Victoria looked at him with a suspicious eye and said: "Cazon is shredded, almost grinded shark meat cooked in a tomato sauce. It doesn't sound good, but after you taste it, all you want inside your empanadas for the rest of your life is Cazon."

"I have had shark steak before, but this is something completely different" said Ray. "It's amazing! I'm not having any other kind of empanadas ever, after trying this. I have to find the wisdom of making Cazon Empanadas."

Everyone attacked the empanadas filled with Cazon first. They had fruits and sweet cantaloupe juice.

Eduardo was moving SCUBA tanks around, placing and spacing them ready to be attached to their buoyancy compensators and breathing regulator sets. The girls and Ray were putting on their wetsuits and tying their hair into ponytails to keep it out of the way.

Chris went below to change into a bathing suit and noticed he had a missed call on his phone from the night before. He picked it up and punched the number.

"Chris?" said Rick over the phone after two rings. It sounded like he was in a tunnel or some confined space with an echo in the background.

"Yes, Rick, encrypted!" answered Chris.

"I hear your friends from the party are still looking for you" Rick said.

"Yeah, we almost ran into them. We don't think they saw us, but they did see the boat. I believe they took off in a hurry to go around to intercept us. It was one of the guys and another one who we have never met" Chris explained.

"What are the chances you and Ray can chase Rodrigo and his gang out here into deeper waters? We'd love to prepare a welcome party for them" Rick said.

"Let me think about that, no promises" replied Chris and hung up. Chris walked back out to the stern deck where Susana and Victoria were on their final gear check and Ray sat with his gear already on the dive platform.

Eduardo helped the girls step down to the platform and Chris reminded them: "Remember, we'll snorkel on shallow water against the current to that point, start our dive there and come back with the current at about thirty feet. Stay on the leeward of the island and it will be an easier swim. Back on the boat with five hundred pounds as always. Have fun ladies!" With that, the girls nodded at each other and entered the water one at a time with a giant stride, kicking their fins as they entered the water. They signaled Eduardo and Ray with a hand patting their heads, turned around and started swimming towards the shallower water breathing through their snorkels.

Ray turned to the side and asked Chris: "What's up with Rick?"

"He wants us to push the party out to them. I told him I would think about it."

"I am starting to feel like Norman Paperman in Kinja trying to play by Kinja rules" said Ray, placing the snorkel in his mouth, sliding in the water face first and swimming to catch up with the girls.

Chris finished strapping his SCUBA gear on, slipped into his fins and went after them. They met about thirty yards from the rocky island, nodded at each other and switched from their snorkels to their regulators to start the dive.

Safe divers always try to get to the deepest part of their dive first. This way they allow more time to dissolve the nitrogen absorbed under pressure into their tissues in shallower waters. Ray emptied his buoyancy compensator and inverted himself with his hands to the side. Chris followed and the girls took their time in upright positions. It's a fun feeling, just freefalling into the deepwater. Ray and Chris kept an eye on the cliff wall and adjusted direction so as not to bounce off it. They also kept looking at the three diving computers strapped to their arms. All of them were exactly at reading depth. Two of them varied slightly on the bottom time remaining. It must have been differences in the algorithm and dive tables calculations. They continued their descend until the first computer showed three dashes and they immediately slowed down by inflating their buoyancy compensators. The second and third computers dashed less than ten feet further. They stopped descending, made their annotations on their slates and started swimming up along the wall to shallower depths.

Large cubera snappers, red and black groupers swam by curious about the new visitors on their reef wall. Both Chris and Ray inspected several holes and crevices on the wall for Lionfish and lobsters. A couple of reef sharks hung in the background about twenty yards off the wall.

Ray took his underwater writing slate where he kept his notes. He wrote the word "Cazon", showed it to Chris and pointed at the sharks behind them. Chris just moved his head slightly right and left trying to keep his mouthpiece as he laughed.

Susana and Victoria were engaged in similar activities searching for invasive species but in shallower waters. Chris and Ray ran into them on the wall at about fifty feet.

They were both looking into a small cave on the wall. Susana turned around when they came up to her and making a sign with three fingers pointing out on both hands pointed towards the small cave. Victoria backed out of the small cave and Ray stuck his head in the cave. From his knife strap inside his leg, he pulled out a short speargun shaft with a trident at one of the ends. He brought it up and inside the cave and came out with a midsize lionfish.

Susana already had pulled out a pair of industrial scissors and carefully began to cut the fish's long spines off at their base. Once all the spines were gone, she pushed what was left of the dead lionfish into a mesh bag. They repeated the procedure two more times as a team and continued their swim up the wall but in the direction of the anchored boat. They didn't see any more lionfish on the swim back to the boat.

Once at the anchor of the old Chris Craft near the beach, one by one, they started swimming up to a depth of fifteen feet. They hung holding the chain of the anchor looking at the beautiful underwater landscape of coral, sponges and fish surrounding them. Ray signaled Susana and Victoria to start ascending towards the boat's platform. Chris and Ray stayed at that depth for a bit longer looking up to see the girls climbing the steps back into the boat. Once the end of the platform was cleared, they swam up to it, took their fins off and climbed the ladder.

The deck of the old Chris Craft got busy once everyone was out of the water. The gear was being disassembled and reassembled for the next dive. Eduardo moved the empty tanks closer to the air compressor for refills. Wetsuits were hung up to drain. Ray took the lionfish out of the mesh bag and started cleaning them. After all the activity started to slow down, captain Giovanni came out from the galley with a tray containing slices of mango and pineapple. "You need some sugar in you guys. That water is still salty." He passed the tray around and everyone grabbed some fruit.

After peeling his wet suit off, Ray went in the galley and started cutting the lionfish into small chunks.

"Captain, can you spare an onion, some limes and parsley?" Ray asked.

"But of course! Here! Giovanni pulled a crate with vegetables and pulled out an onion and parsley. "You know where the limes are."

Ray proceeded to cut the onion and some parsley, then he squeezed about four large limes into the bowl, mixed everything well, covered it and left it in the galley.

The sun felt great on the skin after being in the water for an hour. All the divers were on the sunny side of the deck. Eduardo was filling tanks with the air compressor and Giovanni was in the galley cooking something. A small peñero approached from around the island towards the boat gliding on the short waves. A single short guy on the tiller. Giovanni came out of the galley and saw the peñero approach along the port side of the boat.

"Let's see what they will try to sell us now" said the captain walking over to the rail.

The guy on the peñero pulled three midsize lobsters from bottom of the small boat and showed them to

Giovanni. Giovanni nodded and turned around towards the galley. He came back out a few minutes later and handed the guy on the small boat money in exchange for the three lobsters.

Chris, Ray, Susan and Victoria were already looking over the side and staring at Giovanni.

"Lobster Risotto!" was all he said lifting the three lobsters by their long spines and went back in the galley in a happy mood.

The sun was up, and the deck was starting to warm up. Looking towards the southwestern point of the island. Chris said: "Well, are we ready for another dive? Do we have enough surface time for another dive?"

Susana, Victoria and Ray had been laying out under the sun. They started to move slowly and started scrolling down the different depths in their dive computers.

"How deep are we thinking?" Ray asked.

"Not more than sixty feet" answered Chris.

"I'm good to go!" answered Ray.

"Good here!" followed Susana.

"Good to go!" said Victoria.

They started to get into their wet suits and SCUBA gear again. This time it was warmer under the sun, and it wasn't long before they started to sweat inside their suits.

As they were getting geared up, Chris said: "Let's start our dive as soon as we get in the water and drop down to fifty feet. We'll head out to that point of the island and swim back on the shallows more protected by the island."

Jumping back in the water felt great. The cool water slowly entering the warmth inside the wetsuits feels much better. Everyone adjusted their gear as they entered the water and together, they began their dive. Two small sharks were hanging around the boat's anchor, but they scattered and left when they noticed the divers descending upon them. A minute or two later they reached fifty feet, stabilized their buoyancy and continued southwest towards the tip of Picuda Chica. More small caves and crevices to be checked, but this time they did not find lionfish in them.

After about forty minutes Ray gave the signal to turn around and they slowly started to swim back at a shallower depth. More corals, rocks, small caves, sponges, fish, a spotted moray eel, but not one sea snake. It wasn't long by the time they were back at the anchor and on board the boat. They rinse their wet suits and took freshwater rinse showers after soaping up and jumping in the saltwater. By the time they were done it was early evening. The sun was starting to go down behind the island of Chimana Grande.

Susana and Victoria mixed and served drinks and Ray came out with two packages of saltine crackers and a bowl of ceviche. "Try my Lionfish ceviche."

"Salud!" said Cris with a glass of rum and Coke and lime in his hand as he walked towards the table for some ceviche.

"I have never had Lionfish" said Veronica.

"Neither have I" said Susana.

"You never know until you try it" replied Ray.

They stood around the table with their drinks and dipped the lionfish ceviche out of the bowl with the crackers.

"Another day at the office!" said Chris.

"We'll have dinner in about an hour" came from the captain as he stuck his head out of the galley.

"Susana, I've been meaning to tell you that I believe I saw a marine snake the night we dove inside the cave in La Borracha. I was telling Ray last night about it. I'm glad I remembered" said Chris to Susana who lifted her eyebrows.

"Where? Can you be more specific?" asked Susana.

"When I went out to see if the coast was clear, I saw what I think was a whitish sea snake swimming close to the bottom. I didn't want to turn my light on at the time and I was more concerned with the speedboat hanging out for too long. It was swimming close to the entrance of the cave." If we have time and can go back to make a quick dive there, we may want to try night vision goggles and no light. It's just a hunch. When we all came back out of the cave I didn't see it" Chris explained.

"Cool!" said Susana

"Susana, tell us more about the island of Margarita where you went to school? asked Ray.

Susana went on to explain: "La Isla de Margarita used to be a wonderful place back in the days when I was attending the Universidad de Oriente. The university is situated between the city of Porlamar and the capital of the state, which is La Asuncion. On a any given day you can drive up to the tallest point and find wild roses in the mist or drive down to Playa Parguito and surf some waves. We used to bring our surfboards to school and drive up to Playa Parguito after school. There was nothing but coconut trees from the main road to the beach. Nowadays it is overpopulated with commerce and street vendors. It looks more like a county fair."

"I believe that the fact that the island is a free port has helped the island's economy but is also damaging most of its beauty. There were isolated beaches back in the days. I remember spearfishing at the point off El Tirano and bringing the catch to a lady at a restaurant where she would cook it for us. Those used to be nice days. Today, the island has exploded with hotels, resorts, condominium towers and of course, all the commerce. It's just sad, but I guess that's progress.

"The population has also changed. When I moved there, most retailers were of Arabic or Turkish origin. To-day you hear a thicker population of Russians. I don't know why but can only imagine.

"Anyway, it is still a beautiful island. I just hope we can preserve what's left of its beauty."

They were all sitting outside watching the end of the sunset and the red sky towards the west when Giovanni came out and announced that dinner was ready.

"Get yourself one of the clean plates from the table and follow me, please" Giovanni instructed.

Everyone followed with curiosity as to what Giovanni had up his sleeves this time around. Each one grabbed a plate from the table and one by one stepped inside the gal-ley. Giovanni was serving half a lobster full of butter and garlic on top of a bed of risotto. The aroma was exquisite.

They all sat in aw savoring the delicious meal that the captain had prepared on another beautiful evening in Mochima.

"It's going to be hard to top this one" Ray said and then took another fork full of lobster risotto.

"Captain, what are the rules about fishing inside the park?" Chris asked.

"It is prohibited to fish inside the national park but is not enforced" replied Giovanni. "You see, if they find a speargun, pneumatic or rubber on your boat, the Guarda Costa will take it away and you're supposed to get fined. They'll take it away for sure, but they don't know how to fine you."

"Out here there are fishermen huts on these islands. They are supposed to fish in the waters outside the park, but they can't tell by themselves when they're outside the park. They run their lines and their nets when no one is watching.

"We don't know where that guy that I bought the lobsters from was fishing for them. If I knew he was fishing inside the park I would 've never bought them. When you ask them where they caught them, they point out to sea, but don't tell you where.

"So, without enforcement, there are no rumors or stories to tell or pass to people that they should not fish in the park. I've seen private boats shooting grouper and snapper out here, but what do you do? If you call the Guarda costa, they ignore you. If they're close by, they'll stop by, decommission the spearguns and they continue on their way. What happens to the spearguns? Nobody knows. It's another sad situation, but very realistic. The Guarda Costa station that you all saw when we entered the basin today has three cutters. Only one runs. The other two are on the hard waiting for parts or repairs. It is sad. The only positive problem is that we don't have much traffic around here. During the long weekends and holidays, you'll see more private boats running, but not many hardcore fishermen inside the park, The hardcore run out to the trenches between La Tortuga and Margarita for the big game in thousands of feet of depth, marlin, swordfish, sailfish.

"But enough of me whining. Do you guys want to spend the night here and jump over to Picuda Grande at first light tomorrow? Or would you like to move tonight?" asked Captain Giovanni.

"Captain, all I can tell you right now is that I am stuffed and would prefer to move tomorrow morning" said Ray.

"We can do that!" followed Chris. "We made good progress today. Let's move in the morning. Besides, I kind of like this neighborhood. Do you think back in the days these islands were pirate hideouts and places where they careened their boats?"

"Yes, definitely!" answered Captain Giovanni. "You must remember that pearls were harvested around the island of Margarita, so it was a place that was regularly plundered by pirates like Calico Jack, Charles Vane and Henry Morgan. The Royal Navy never had enough ships to chase them all the way down here without leaving the waters of Barbados, St Lucia and the Grenadines unprotected.

Plus, they also had to be aware of the Spanish ships sailing from the coast.

"The Spanish traders and galleons would load gold, silver, cocoa, coffee in ports like Puerto La Cruz, La Guaira, Puerto Cabello and Maracaibo. Fully loaded ships sailing back to Europe via Hispaniola or Cuba were easy prays for the pirates. There is a lot of history about the pirates' days around here. These islands were the perfect place to hide and ambush other ships. I don't know about hidden treasures, but I'm sure there are stories about that as well. I have always heard rumors about a small fleet of pirate ships running onto troubled weather between some of these islands and sinking. The ships were heavily laden after raiding Port of Spain in Trinidad and Porlamar on the island of Margarita. One must remember that none of these islands had lighthouses or villages with fires burning at night in those days. Because of the deep water, by the time they were able to see an island at night, it might have been too late. There is no warning of shallower waters or bordering reefs. But it's only rumors you hear.

"You'll still find forts and ruins that were built by the Spanish to protect cities and ports. There were forts in Margarita, Puerto La Cruz, Cumana, Puerto Cabello and Maracaibo. Historical records are hard to find around here, but these were ideal waters for piracy."

"This is all very interesting, but I hear a hammock calling my name" said Ray as he got up from the chair. "I'll probably have nightmares with Sea Hags and shipwrecks. I will see you guys in the morning. Good night!"

"Good night, Ray!" replied the captain.

Chris sat with captain Giovanni a little longer listening to stories before retiring for the night. He then lay inside the hammock trying to come up with a plan to wash the smugglers out to sea and still accomplish the phase of the projects they were involved in. It was going to be a tough one.

CHAPTER 16

Wilfredo and Jairo drove past Lecherias and around the neighborhoods with all the canals to reach the marina Americo Vespucio. Lecherias is a suburb of Puerto La Cruz. It has always been a mixture of residential homes with vacation homes and hotels split from Puerto La Cruz by neighborhoods built around man-made canals. A very long time ago it was mostly vacation homes. As it grew and people wanted to get away from the city, they moved out to Lecherias. Nowadays one will find a mixture of full-time residents and part-time vacationers in one place. The areas with the canals are probably the properties with the highest value of the zone. It could have been a beautiful resort area like Hilton Head in South Carolina or Ocean Reef in Florida, but now golf courses that were never finished have dried up, the grounds and facilities maintenance keep getting deferred. Marinas were lacking services. The original touristic resort planning, and ideas were great, but without follow up and funding it's not gaining prestige nor value.

They pulled up to the parking area and got out of the old Land Cruiser. Their first stop was at the fuel dock, but the hoses were locked and there was no one around. They walked down to the marina offices, and they also were closed for the day. Then they went around to the pub next door for another beer. The pub was starting to fill with people. They ordered two Polar beers. While drinking and arguing over what to do, Jairo's phone rang.

"Si Jefe!" Jairo answered the phone.

"Have you found them? Have you found the gringos?" asked Rodrigo Escalante.

"No Jefe, but we saw the boat they were in before, the one you and Wilfredo stopped by the other night. They were fueling at the marina across from us about an hour ago and loading food. We think they saw us, and they went back out. We lost them by the time we came around to the marina" replied Jairo.

"We're going back out there to speak with that captain tomorrow night. Make sure the boat has enough fuel to search the islands" Rodrigo ordered.

"Si Jefe!" Jairo responded, but the line was already dead.

Jairo looked at Wilfredo and said: "Let's get the boat ready."

"It's going to have to wait until morning. The fuel docks are closed now" said Wilfredo.

They ordered another beer.

Rodrigo Escalante sat on the patio in his villa by the hills drinking aguardiente and wearing a silk robe. He was afraid of making the next call to his boss. He was trying to come up with an excuse since he didn't want to travel back down to the coast and search the waters tonight. The more he thought about the trouble these gringos had created for him, the more upset he became.

"Get me another drink!" he ordered one of the girls sitting next to him.

Rodrigo was thinking about taking both girls to his bedroom and having his way with them when the phone on the table rang. He shook his thoughts out of his head and picked up the phone.

"What's this I hear that you can't find them?" shouted Cecilia Machado at the other end of the call.

"Si, Jefa! The boys saw the boat fueling up and loading at one of the marinas, but by the time they got there the boat was gone. They didn't see the gringos onboard, but we believe the captain may know where they went. We are going out there tomorrow to find them."

"Why not now Rodrigo? What are you waiting for? Are you busy with another one of your parties?" asked Cecilia with sarcasm.

"No Jefa! It's just that we need to fuel the boat, and it will be easier to find them during the day. The navigation around those islands at night is tricky."

"Bring me those gringos Rodrigo" Cecilia shouted over the phone and hung up.

"I hate this witch! shouted Rodrigo.

Rodrigo slammed the phone on the table, took another shot of Aguardiente and got up from the chair. At that same moment, his legs trembled like he had been running all day. For a second, he thought someone had laced his favorite alcoholic drink, but then he remembered his past. As a teenager, Rodrigo had experience two earthquakes when he lived in Cali, Colombia. This felt just like it. When he looked at the glasses on the table still with some fluid, they were also trembling. He looked up at a lamp under the overhang and it was swinging side to side. It was indeed an earthquake, not very strong, but an earthquake.

The mountains of Venezuela are in constant motion. It's not a motion that can be measured by the way we measure time. But by geological time. There the mountains get pushed and pressured by three tectonic plates: the Nazca, the Caribbean and the Atlantic plates. Every now and then there are tremors and earthquakes generated by that motion. This was one of those tremors that came without prediction.

"An earthquake, that's all I need now" thought Rodrigo.

The two girls sitting on a couch nearby looked at each other in panic, but soon realized it was just a short tremor. As fast as it came, it was gone. It wasn't followed by another one, which sometimes happened.

"Bring yourselves and another bottle of Aguardiente" Rodrigo told the girls and walked inside the house.

Wilfredo and Jairo felt the tremor walking towards the old Land Cruiser. They felt it at a lower magnitude but they both blamed it on the beers they had earlier, so they didn't make anything out of it. They climbed inside the Land Cruiser and drove back to Santa Fe for the night but stopped for more beers on the outskirts of Puerto La Cruz. On the drive back to Santa Fe with a buzz from all the beers they encountered rain, but without a driver side window, they got soaked in minutes by the water.

CHAPTER 17

An orange glow started illuminating the sky in the east as the sun was about to rise. Chris could hear Susana and Victoria in their usual happy giggling moods and helping Captain Giovanni with breakfast preparation. He noticed the smell of coffee brewing in the air.

Good morning sunshine! said Victoria holding a glass of orange juice in front of Chris. "I know you don't drink coffee."

"Good morning, Victoria!" said Chris. "Thank you!".

Ray had been up for a while checking gear, looking at charts and getting organized for the day.

Captain Giovanni had prepared breakfast burritos stuffed with scrambled eggs cooked with onion, tomato and bell pepper. He had also prepared a tray of fresh fruits including grapefruit, orange, cantaloupe and watermelon.

Ray said: "I believe the cement boat wreck will be a good dive site to include in the analysis of invasive species. It lies at a depth of eighty-five feet. We should do at least one dive there and then move to Picuda Grande for our afternoon shallower dive. It's only a run of less than five miles to Picuda Grande. That will be plenty of time for a good surface interval. What do you think?"

"That would be great" said Victoria. "I never dove that wreck site before."

"You'll like it!" chimed in Susana. "It's different.".

"I'm good with that plan. I'm liking it already," said Chris.

"It's a plan then! said Ray.

After breakfast everyone started moving in different directions, preparing gear, getting into wetsuits, starting computers, loading batteries and all the motions of a pre-dive scenario.

Ray said to Susana: "You haven't had a chance to use your underwater scooters. This might be a good site to run them."

"What a great idea! They'll let us cover more area" Susana said and went to prepare the underwater scooters with Victoria.

With the help of Eduardo all the gear was loaded into the inflatable rigid tender. Once everyone was onboard, Eduardo released the painter from the boat cleat and walked with the line inside the tender. He let the tender drift from the boat and turned it into a northeast heading towards the wreck site. The plan was for Eduardo to stay nearby with the tender while they dove into the wreck and then pick them up after they surfaced. It was a better plan than swimming over two miles to the wreck and two miles back.

Once they were over the cement boat wreck and had checked their gear, all four of them rolled backwards into the water. Susana and Victoria swam back to the tender where Eduardo handed them each a blue underwater scooter.

Chris and Ray were approaching the bottom when they started to hear the buzzing sound of the underwater scooters. They all met at the bow of the shipwreck which sat in deeper water.

Susana and Victoria started on the port side of the wreck while Chris and Ray took the starboard side. Not ten feet from the bow, all the way under the hull of the wreck, Susana noticed a fissure between the wreck and the sand on the bottom, almost like a natural ledge. She let her underwater scooter hang from the clipped line to her vest and took a small flashlight out of her buoyancy compensator pocket. Victoria saw her out of the corner of her mask and turned back towards her.

Susana laid down on the sandy bottom and shined her flashlight into the fissure. Inside at the bottom lying on the sand were what looked like black or brown rocks that did not belong there. They were not the right color or type of rock. She carefully took the spot of her flashlight all around the inside of the fissure to check for other inhabitants. Not seeing any other creatures inside, she carefully stuck her arm inside the fissure and tried to reach one of the strange rocks. She reached one of the rocks, pulled it out and handed it to Victoria who was already pulling out her flashlight to study the rock. It felt heavy. Susana reached back inside the fissure and pulled four more rocks and placed them inside a small mesh bag. Victoria placed the one she was handed inside the mesh bag as well. They continued along the bottom port side of the wreck looking into holes and cuts in the steel hull.

The shipwreck had become an artificial reef. Parrotfish and wrasse in multiple colors stared and took off curiously watching the divers swim by. Starfish, coral, sponges and crabs in different shades of reds and browns adorned the steel structure. Small groupers and snappers swam in and out of the portholes of the hull. So far everything they ran into was very native to these waters.

Towards the stern of the ship two propellers were half buried in the sand as if the ship had run hard aground. More fish ran in and out of the bottom of the wreck. Chris and Ray met Susana and Victoria at the stern by the propellers. Ray saw the small bag hanging from Susana's gear and held it for a bit looking at it. He threw it up to feel its weight and nodded at Susana.

Chris signaled the divers to start moving up towards the deck of the wreck. Once they cleared the stern, they could see all the cement bags in the cargo bay of the ship stacked up. Some of the bags had moved or fallen off a stack and were laying in odd positions. It was like time had stopped, the cement sacks had lost their paper bags and had dried up. If it wasn't for all the fish and invertebrates everywhere, it would've e looked more like a ship at a dock waiting to be unloaded. They swam over the open cargo bay and then up onto the bridge level where there were hatches and doors they could swim through and go inside the bridge.

The inside of the bridge was more deteriorated or had suffer more during the sinking, Cables and pipes were all over in no order. Parts of the steering wheel and throttle controls were still attached to the bridge console. Cables hung from everywhere. All the glasses of the bridge windshield were gone. Overall, the structure of the ship was still intact. Ray tried to enter through the steps leading to lower decks under the bridge, but there were too many obstructions to fit. They swam out of the bridge and up onto the roof where some of the antennas were still standing attached. From that level they could observe the entire wreck from bow to stern. They were now at about fifty feet in depth. Ray started pointing at the pressure gauge turning it around for the others to see. The rest repeated the motion. They were all at about one thousand pounds of air.

Chris jumped down to the bow deck and the rest followed him. On the bow deck the windlass and some of the anchor chains were still attached to the wreck. Chris signaled everyone to start their ascend. Together they swam to about fifteen feet of depth and they could already hear the outboard of the tender above coming towards them. They hung there for a few more minutes and then surfaced, one by one, with the help of Eduardo, undid their gear, but kept their mask and fins to kick themselves onto the tender.

Once they were all inside the inflatable rigid tender with all their gear secured, Eduardo pointed the small boat back to Picuda Chica. On the way, Susana pulled the mesh bag with the rocks she had collected under the wreck. She looked at them and then passed them around for the others to see and touch.

"What do you make of them Susana?" asked Ray over the sound of the small outboard.

"I don't know." answered Susana. "They are not biological. They also feel heavier than your usual coral rocks, and the coloration is unusual. I want to clean them and figure out what they are. I just hope they are not radioactive. I don't have any means nor access to a Geiger counter."

Chris smiled and said: "I don't think you'll find radiation. Did you notice all the living organisms around and inside that shipwreck? If there was radiation, it would have to be minimal. Otherwise, the shipwreck would be desolated."

Eduardo brought the tender and they tied it up on the stern to unload all their gear. Once the gear was unloaded, Eduardo untied the stern line of the tender and let out as much as he could of the bow line before retying it. The tender floated now about twenty feet from the old Chris Craft and ready to be towed.

"Everyone good? Did you all have a good dive? "Giovanni asked while the group began to disassemble their gear and hook up fresh air tanks.

Everyone nodded.

"Yes!" said Susana as she raised her small mesh bag with the rocks inside.

Giovanni walked up to her, took the mesh bag and looked at its contents. "They don't seem alive, so they 're okay to be on my boat in these waters." he said with a smile.

"I'm glad to hear that I'm not alive Captain" said Ray with some sarcasm.

Everyone laughed and Giovanni climbed on the bridge shouting: "Secure your gear. Eduardo let's get ready to weigh anchor. We're moving to Picuda Grande."

He started the engines and let them warm up for a few minutes before the sound of the anchor chain coming on board could be heard.

After peeling their wet suits and hanging them, Susana stepped inside towards the galley and the rest of the group went to join the captain on the bridge. Once the anchor was up on the boat and secured, the captain turned the boat and headed northeast towards Picuda Grande.

PICUDA GRANDE

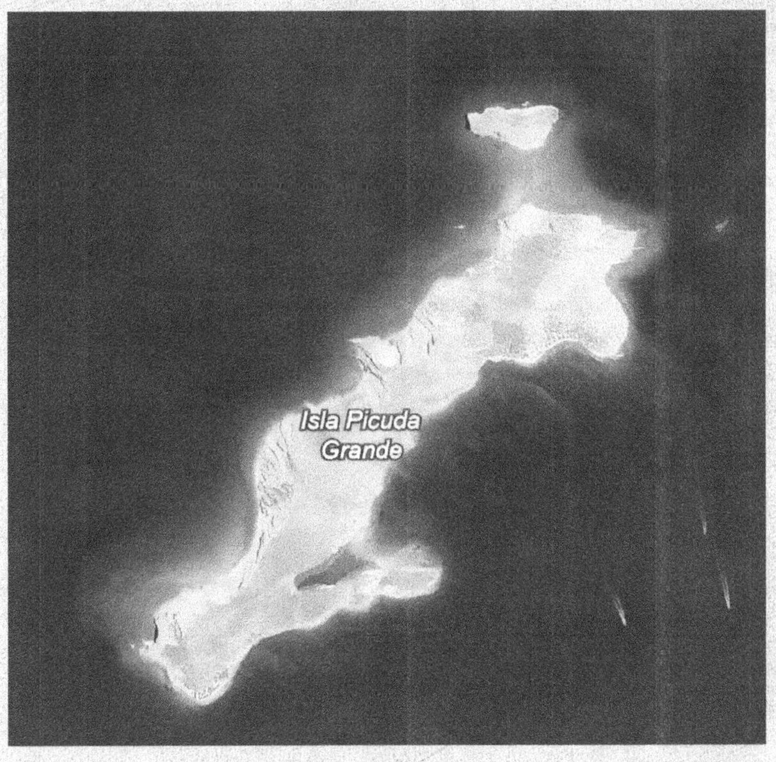

CHAPTER 18

On the run towards Picuda Grande Susana had brought out a few plastic containers from the galley that Eduardo had provided to her. She also found a large bottle of vinegar and two small boxes of baking soda. She cleared the wet table in the center of the wet stern deck and placed the plastic trays next to each other. She then proceeded to mix solutions for each one of them pouring water from the hose used for rinsing their gear. Carefully taking the small rocks out of the mesh and placing them inside the first acidic solution of vinegar, she looked at her dive watch to keep time on the immersion of the small rocks. Happy with her setup, she went to join the rest of the group on the bridge.

The run to Picuda Grande was only four and a half miles, which they made quickly despite going against the wind and the currents. Captain Giovanni eased up on the throttles as they made the turn towards a small basin with a shallow tidal lagoon at the end.

"We must be careful inside here" said the captain as he maneuvered the boat. "There are shallow rocks on both sides and an outcropping of rocks in the center of that small cove. I am going to go around those submerged rocks on the port side and anchor the boat inside that cove. It's very peaceful there. There's great snorkeling on both sides of the cove and you can walk in shallow water all the way up that lagoon. Hopefully, we'll have enough of a breeze to keep the bugs away."

"Eduardo, let's get ready to drop the anchor" shouted the captain down the companionway.

Once the boat was lined up in the center of the cove, he signaled Eduardo to start letting the anchor and chain out. The chain rattled the boat as it dropped to the bottom. Giovanni reversed the engines to make sure the anchor positioned itself and would catch. Once he felt the tension of the anchor digging at the bottom, he brought the engines to neutral.

"Welcome to Picuda Grande" he said as he turned around to face the others with a smile. He let the engines run for a few minutes to cool down and then shut them off. The calm of the water inside the cove and light breeze running between the two hills of the island made it feel like the best place in the world to relax and take a nap.

"What are you cooking here?" asked Ray as he joined Susana at the wet table.

"I'm trying to remove some of the oxidation and growth on these rocks. I still have about another half hour to go on the first bath" explained Susana while slightly agitating the tray with the rocks back and forth.

Eduardo came out of the galley with ham and cheese sandwiches and a large plate of fresh fruit. He placed the trays on the table and said: "Lunch! buen provecho!"

They all attacked the trays with the sandwiches and the sliced pineapple, cantaloupe and watermelon. Appetite is one of those things that diving generates in an exaggerated manner. It must be the exercise of constant motion while breathing clean filtered air under pressure.

Of course, after feasting there were no other results but the attraction of the body towards a hammock slightly swinging with the motion of a boat. The light breeze and the quiet sounds of small waves slapping the shore with a few seagulls chirping in the background made it easier to give up.

Susana's dive watch chimed three times before she turned the alarm off. She stepped down from the hammock and walked towards the wet table with the plastic containers. "It must be working" she said quietly as to not wake the others up from their naps. The solution around the small rocks had turned reddish. She lifted the tray with the rocks and moved it slightly to stir the acidic solution. Then, she picked up the rocks with her fingers and placed them into the next tray that contained fresh water for a short rinse. She also started rubbing and hitting the small rocks with each other. Fragments of the black and reddish pieces covering the rocks started to crumple apart revealing a yellowish core. After removing the black pieces as much as she could, she placed the rocks in the solution with baking soda to neutralize any acid left in them. She could not believe what she was looking at.

Chris was getting up from the hammock and stretching when he noticed Susana's expression on her face while looking closer into the plastic container. He walked up to the wet table where Susana was standing and asked her: "What have you got there?"

"I don't know! Can you please look at these rocks and tell me I'm not seeing what I'm seeing?" said Susana still in shock.

Chris came around the table and took a closer look at the plastic container with the rocks at the bottom. He stuck his index finger and thumb and extracted one of the rocks for a closer look.

"I have seen some of these off the coast of Florida and Cartagena" Chris said while still looking at the rock. It's hard to confirm right now how old these are. You would have to clean them some more, but I believe what you have here are Doubloons. It's hard to tell right now weather these are Spanish or Portuguese. We would have to take a closer and cleaner look at the shields, but you can see parts of it on this one." He handed it to Susana who still had an expression of shock.

"Let me take a look at the others" said Chris pulling another rock out of the solution.

By now Victoria and Ray had joined them around the table and Susana was handing them the rocks that Chris had pulled out of the last container.

"They could very well be Doubloons," said Ray. "Here is some good research to be done once you can clean them and find their provenance. I'm going to go and put my money on Spanish Doubloons. Do you see here on this side of this one, you can barely read the letters HISP?"

Ray handed the coin back to Susana and asked: "I wonder how those coins made it under that shipwreck?" Are we thinking the same thing?

"It could very well be" said Chris.

"What? What? I can't read minds," asked Susana excited to hear what they were thinking.

Ray smiled and said: "It could be that the cement shipwreck ended up on top of another much older shipwreck. The chances are slim, but possible."

"Do you think so?" asked Victoria.

"We need to go back and dive that wreck again" said Susana.

"Wait a minute, slow down there, Speedy. We just got here, said Chris. "Let's make two dives here to complete the transect and then we'll discuss if we want to dive that shipwreck again. I understand this is all very exciting, but we need to finish our field work before jumping on another quest. Let's think some more about this."

"Okay! Okay! But then we'll make a couple of dives on that shipwreck" said Susana excited about their find.

"It will probably have to be tomorrow. Let's make a dive on the northwest side of Picuda Grande this afternoon and the southeast side tonight. We'll ask Eduardo to drop us at the point and we'll drift dive with the current" said Ray. "Is that okay with everyone?"

Everyone agreed.

"I need about ten minutes to pick all this up and put it away before I can go" said Susana.

"Not a problem! We'll wait for you," said Ray.

They started getting their gear ready while waiting for Susana.

"Eduardo, can you take us to the northern point? We'll drift back into the cove" asked Ray.

"No problem!" said Eduardo as he went to tie up the tender behind the swim platform.

They loaded their gear and were off to the northern point of the island. When they rounded the cove and were on the northwest side of the island, Chris asked Eduardo: "Can you drop us at that cove between the island and that rock to the north?"

"No problem!" was Eduardo's response as he pointed the tender in the direction of the shallow turquoise waters of the northern cove. Eduardo eased the tender into the shallow water, turned the outboard off and lifted the lower unit out of the water. They glided into the shallow waters and jumped off the inflatable before it hit the rocks underwater. They pulled their gear out of the inflatable and double checked that they had everything.

Chris and Ray pushed the inflatable back towards deeper water once Eduardo had climbed back in. Eduardo started the outboard and drifted out of the cove waiting for them to go underwater. Once all the heads were underwater, he turned and steered the tender back to the old Chris Craft.

Chris, Ray, Susana and Victoria started their dive in shallow water and swam out and down until they reached about sixty feet in depth. Then, they continued drifting with the current, but with the wall of the island on their left side. They were all thinking about the coins back in the boat. their provenance, the wreck, what to do next, were some of the thoughts running through their heads as they were diving along the wall of the island.

Along the wall of the island, they inspected more of the similar small caves and crevices for invasive species. Chris was facing the surface clearing water out of his mask. When he was done and turned his face back forward, there was a thick green moray eel looking at him inches from the faceplate of his mask. It opened its mouth and closed it all in one motion and then took off to one of the sides. Chris followed it as it seemed to be swallowed by a pile of rocks. Ray just kept looking at Chris through the whole encounter with the eel. Chris lifted his shoulders and opened his hands while looking at Ray.

They continued with their late afternoon dive enjoying the brightness of the sun rays penetrating from the southwest. They spotted lobsters and crabs staring at them from the inside of more caves and crevices. Many parrotfish, a few small snappers and groupers were some of the fish that swam by with curiosity. Top hats, damsels, butterflies and surgeons hung around the rocks and corals along with Spanish hogfish, tangs and rock beauties. A pair of French angel fish were along for the ride following them.

Visibility was over eighty feet on that side of the island. The current pushing them at about a knot, or a knot and a half made it easy to swim with it as well as stopping when they needed to. A large black grouper came to check them out from deeper waters and then turned and went back into the deep. A male hog snapper with its black stripe over each eye swam towards them and then took off. A school of sergeant majors became protective of their area and got excited as they got closer.

It was a very pleasant dive until they reached the south-western point where the current from both sides of the inland merged. It was time to start kicking against to get out of the northern current and swim against the southern current towards the cove.

As a group they decided to go into shallower waters where the currents were not so strong. They swam at about twenty feet of depth until they reached the southern tip of the cove where captain Giovanni had anchored the boat. Once at the tip they surfaced and continued towards the boat in a more relaxed swim. By the time they reached the boat, the sun was behind the hill of the island. Eduardo had tied the inflatable tender on the port side of the boat giving them more room to come out of the water with their gear.

"We should have taken the underwater scooters" said Victoria as soon as she was out of the water on the swim platform.

"I thought about suggesting that earlier, but I didn't expect such a long-distance swim against the current," replied Ray while still floating behind the swim platform waiting for Susana to climb out of the water.

"Always plan for the worst" said Chris.

They climbed out of the water, put their gear away and peeled off their wetsuits. The wind had picked up and the sun was no longer shining on the deck, so it became cooler faster. They rinsed their wet suits, themselves and then dried off.

Giovanni came out with a tray of cheese, pepperoni, salami and prosciutto. "It's starting to look like happy hour around here."

Susana and Victoria went to check on the coins after putting all their gear away.

Ray went to put some music on, and it was Chris' turn to prepare the official happy hour beverages for today.

Eduardo started moving empty tanks closer to the air compressor and replacing the empty spots with full tanks. You could hear the compressor already running and building up the pressure.

They gathered around the table where the container with the coins and the tray of cold cuts were. Jimmy Buffet's "A Pirate Looks at Forty" was playing out of the speakers on the boat. Chris raised a glass: "Salud!"

"Cheers!" replied Ray.

"Salud, Amor y Dinero!" said Susana, raising her glass and holding a coin up in the air.

They all laughed, as Jimmy started singing: " ...how there he watched the men who rode you, switch from sails to steam and in your belly, you hold the treasures few have ever seen. Most of them dream..."

"That's a sign!" said Victoria, still with a smile on her face.

"Alright! Alright! I can't wait to go and dive that shipwreck too" said Ray. "But let's just do our last dive here in a couple of hours. It'll be night by then. We'll ask Eduardo to drop us up there and we'll come back at about forty feet of water directly to the cove and the boat. At first light, we'll ask the captain to move us back to Picuda Chica. We can dive into the wreck by midmorning.

Chris raised his glass and said: "Excelente!".

They nibbled on the cold cuts and made small talk about wrecks, treasures, and ships for the next hour or so while listening to the music.

In between songs and the noise of the compressor kicking in and out, Ray heard a noise far away that didn't seem to belong with the rest of the noises. He went inside to turn the music off. When he came out, he asked Eduardo to shut off the compressor for a few minutes.

In the distance they could hear the familiar noise of the speedboat approaching the island at high speed and pounding the waves.

"Captain, let's go dark!" Chris told Giovanni, who proceeded to a switch panel and started turning all the lights off.

Ray was already retrieving the bag of goodies they had received from General Pineda and placed it on the wet table of the deck.

Chris grabbed one of the Glocks out of the bag, checked the magazine and made sure there was a round in the chamber. "Captain!" Chris said pulling the other Glock out of the bag. When Chris raised his head, he saw Captain Giovanni standing there and holding a shortened shotgun.

"I'm good to go!" said the captain.

"Ray?" Chris offered the gun to Ray.

"I hate guns" said Ray, and he pulled one of the tactical knives, a bunch of the heavy-duty cable ties and folded them inside his cargo shorts' pockets.

Chris took the night vision monocular out and put it over his head. "You go high, I'll go low" he told Ray.

"Girls, hide and stay quite!" he said as he turned towards the inflatable tender.

Ray climbed up to the upper deck. Chris pulled himself and the inflatable forward towards the portside cleat where the tender was tied to. He was looking at the horizon and the tip of the island when he saw the speedboat cruising past the point heading east. The speedboat was halfway past the island when they heard its engines slow down. Chris could see the boat turning through the night vision monocular.

"Here we go! It's showtime!" was all that Chris said and the dark boat went silent.

CHAPTER 19

Rodrigo Escalante woke up in the afternoon with a terrible hangover and a pounding headache. The last thing he remembered was being on the phone with Cecilia Machado, the Witch of the Mountain. He wanted to go back to sleep when he thought about Cecilia. He sat on the bed trying to gain enough balance to stand up. Slowly he walked to the bathroom and into the shower. He stood under a cold shower for what seemed like hours and trying not to think too much. He was just going through the motions. He got dressed and tried to step out onto the terrace but turned around and started looking for his sunglasses. He walked slowly towards a table where the girls were having breakfast and sat down. His head was pounding. He looked at both girls and without a word served himself coffee from a carafe on the table. After two cups of coffee, he could still taste the Aguardiente from the night before. He just sat there trying not to move, trying not to think, just breathing slowly. He tried to eat some of the sliced fruits that had been served on the table, but things were not getting any better. He ordered scrambled eggs, bacon, toast and fried potatoes.

The greasy breakfast seemed to help his hangover, but not enough. He asked one of the girls to get him some cocaine for his headache. The girl went back to the room and came out holding a small mirror with several lines of cocaine and a short glass straw. Rodrigo inhaled a couple of lines and just sat there for another while before he picked up the phone.

"Jairo, is the boat ready?" Rodrigo asked, trying not to shout.

"Si jefe! Listo! Whenever you're ready" answered Jairo.

"I'll be on my way in a few minutes" said Rodrigo before ending the call.

Rodrigo took a deep breath and tried to stand up but fell back on the chair where he was sitting. He sat there for another while and snored a few more lines of cocaine. Finally, he got the strength to get up and start walking out to the driveway where his driver was waiting. The driver saw him walking slowly towards the Nissan SUV and ran to open the rear passenger door. Rodrigo climbed into the seat slowly so as not to move his head too suddenly. When his driver slammed the door right next to him, only bad words came out at a very low volume.

"Santa Fe! Go slow, please" Rodrigo told the driver.

Every time the driver accelerated, stopped or drove over a pothole on the road, Rodrigo felt like it was the end of the world, and his head was going to explode. By the time they had driven past El Naranjo and entering Santa Fe, he was starting to feel better, and his headache was less pounding.

"Let's drive down to the coast where the boys keep the boats in Bahia de Los Coquitos" Rodrigo told the driver. He was starting to recognize his own voice.

Rodrigo's cellphone chimed and he looked at the screen, The Witch of the Mountain.

"Si jefa!" he answered.

"Did you find them? Did you find esos putos gringos? I want them now" he heard Cecilia Machado's voice, and his head pounded again.

"No jefa! Not yet. We are just starting to look for them on the islands. We are sure they are diving the islands" Rodrigo responded.

"Find them and bring them to me today, Rodrigo, no more excuses. Don't make me fly over there to straighten your mess. Stop partying and get to work."

"Si jefa! I'll keep you posted" Rodrigo tried to answer but the call had ended.

By the time his driver pulled up to the parking area of Bahia de Los Coquitos, it was already late afternoon. At least he didn't have to deal with the heat and the sun of the middle of the afternoon. He climbed down from the SUV and walked to the edge of the cliff to see if the boat was there. Not seeing the boat, he pulled his phone out and punched Wilfredo's number.

"I'm here at the cove. Where are you?" Rodrigo spoke as Jairo answered the phone.

"We are at the fisherman's wharf next to the Club Nautico restaurant. We're still getting fuel and oil. It'll be easier for you to board here. I was trying to tell you earlier, but you hung up the phone" Jairo said.

Rodrigo finished the call without saying a word, walked back to the SUV and got in.

"Club Nautico restaurant at the fisherman's wharf. Vamos!"

The driver backed out of the parking area and drove east and then northeast for half a mile. On the first four or five blocks there were beach mansions covering the coast. On the three blocks that followed, there were small fishermen houses on both sides hugging the road. Just past the Ice distributor and the co-op market there was the wharf with fishermen pangas or peñeros as they call them around here. The white and orange speedboat stuck out like a sore thumb.

The driver stopped the SUV in front of the speedboat that was tied to the wharf by the stern and its bow anchored. A long hose that came out of a fuel truck went to the boat fuel intake hose. Wilfredo was loading two gallons of oil onto the boat.

Rodrigo climbed on the boat, sat on the side passenger seat and said: "Let's go!"

"Si jefe! We're almost done refueling" replied Jairo. "Vamos!" he told Wilfredo.

Wilfredo pulled the fuel hose and handed it to the fuel truck driver who handed him the bill. Wilfredo pulled a wad of bills from his pocket and paid the truck driver.

"One thing we still have going for us is the government subsidized fuel prices" Wilfredo thought to himself. He climbed back on the boat, closed the engine cover and started the boat engines.

Rodrigo's head almost fell off his shoulders when Wilfredo started the engines. The pounding headache was back.

Jairo untied the stern line and climbed forward to retrieve the small anchor and place it inside the anchor locker. Wilfredo bumped the engines forward and Jairo almost lost his footing. Jairo just stared at Wilfredo.

Once Jairo was on the stern seat, Wilfredo pushed the throttles and the boat's bow came up and then down on a plane.

"Let's start looking around La Borracha and work our way back" Wilfredo shouted over the noise of the engines at Rodrigo. Rodrigo just nodded and closed his eyes thinking it would help with his pounding headache.

They made the eighteen-mile run to La Borracha as the sun was setting over the west. Rodrigo had his eyes closed most of the trip. Jairo and Wilfredo didn't say a word. The noise of the engines and the wind moving fast over the cockpit made it more difficult to communicate without shouting at each other.

Wilfredo slowed down between El Borracho and La Borracha, and slowly rounded the large island looking into every cove and beach for the old Chris Craft. Next, they crossed over to the Chimana islands. They rounded Chimana del Oeste and came back south past Playa El Saco and Playa Puinare. They turned east, going in between the larger Chimana islands and past Las Playuelas and Isla El Faro. The sun had settled, and it was starting to get dark. The islands seemed like large shadows of monsters staring at them.

At night, one of the first things that go in the human eye is depth perception. The islands looked much closer than they really were. It was almost like they were trying to hug them or squeeze them.

Wilfredo steered the speed boat between Playa Cachicamo and Picuda Chica but didn't see any boats inside any of the coves, or at least not large enough for the Chris Craft boat. Finally, they headed northeast towards Picuda Grande. Wilfredo decided to run on the southern side of the island and go around to its northern side. They were halfway along the island when Jairo looked back and saw the dim anchor light of a boat inside the cove.

Wilfredo turned around! Shouted Jairo at Wilfredo while pointing at the light inside the cove.

Wilfredo saw the dim light and turned the boat around towards the cove. All Rodrigo was able to do was close his eyes and hang on to the passenger seat.

Three hundred yards from the dim light, Wilfredo started to bring the throttles up to bring the boat off plane and slow the boat down. Now they could see the silhouette of the old Chris Craft against the island in the dark. Wilfredo slowly glided towards the starboard side of the Chris Craft. Jairo grabbed a flashlight from a small watertight compartment.

CHAPTER 20

Chris saw the speedboat slowing down and gliding towards the starboard side of the old Chris Craft. He started the small engine on the tender and untied it from the cleat of the boat. He then turned the boat around making half a circle around behind the Chris Craft and came sideways into the stern of the speedboat.

"Where are the gringos?" Jairo shouted at Giovanni with a small flashlight from the speedboat pointed at the captain's face.

With a flat hand moving across his neck, the captain signaled the speedboat to cut their engines because he couldn't hear a word they were saying over the noise.

Jairo turned and told Wilfredo: "Turn the engines off."

When Wilfredo turned the engines off, they heard a loud clang on the stern of the boat.

Chris had landed the small tender on top of the swimming platform of the speedboat. At the same time Ray jumped from above and landed with an arm on Jairo's shoulder and his two feet on the deck of the cockpit. Jairo went straight face down to the deck and Ray already had a knife tip at Wilfredo's neck.

Chris was covering Ray with the Glock and captain Giovanni had his shotgun pointed at Rodrigo, who was in shock and had raised his hands over his shoulders. It all happened so fast that he didn't have a chance to stand up from the passenger bucket seat.

Ray tightened the heavy-duty cable ties around their wrists and laid them face down on the deck of the speedboat while Chris moved the tender back in the water and secured it to the speedboat. Chris came over the engine cover of the speedboat and helped Ray to lift the handcuffed boys into the long stern seat. He also threw a couple of docking lines at Giovanni.

"Who do we have here?" Chris asked, looking at Wilfredo, Jairo and Rodrigo.

"That witch Machado is going to have your balls for breakfast," said Rodrigo with his head down. The headache was getting worse by the minute now.

Chris and Ray searched the boat and found automatic weapons and handguns.

"Let's go for a ride" Chris said as he climbed into the Chris Craft. "I'll be right back."

Chris went after his phone and called Rick to warn him that they were coming to them. He then stepped back down on the speedboat.

By now, the girls had come out and were looking around at the situation.

"Are you ready for a reception?" Chris said on the phone to Rick.

"Let's party!" was all that Rick said.

"I'm bringing the party to you," responded Chris.

Ray knew what was going on, but Giovanni and the girls were in the dark looking at each other. Chris put his phone away in one of his shorts pockets and asked Giovanni to drop the lines on the boat.

"We'll be back in two hours," Chris said to Giovanni.

Chris started the loud engines and backed out of the cove with the tender tied closely. As they started leaving the cove Ray let more line out on the tender and the speedboat went into a plane. He steered the speedboat around the southern tip of the island and then pointed it on a north heading.

Once the reflection from the lights on the mainland diminished, he lowered the night vision monocular that was still on his head. He could now see clearly for a longer distance. Anything with a heat signal would appear in bright red and oranges across his view. He turned around a few times to check on the tender under tow behind the speedboat. He saw the orange outboard thirty feet out bouncing up and down on the wake.

"This night vision technology is amazing. I feel like Doc Ford up there by Gumbo Limbo on Tarpon Bay" shouted Chris to Ray over the noise of the engines.

Ray nodded but kept his eyes fixed on the three men sitting on the stern seat with their hands tied behind their backs.

After twenty minutes Chris brought the engine throttles down and started cruising at a slower speed. Out of nowhere he noticed four heat signatures on the view of the night vision monocular. They were moving at high speed towards him. Chris couldn't tell what he was seeing until they were about a hundred yards out. Four black sixteen feet inflatable boats with four and five men dressed in fully black uniforms and full-face head covers. They all wore low profile automatic flotation devices and shoulder holsters with guns, combat knives and additional ammo. Every other one wore a set of night vision goggles. He counted two men holding automatic rifles on every boat.

"This must be the reception party" Chris said to Ray as he brought the speedboat to neutral to let it slide on the swells. He lifted the night vision monocular from his face to his head and realized how impressive the night vision set worked. Now it was very dark, and he could barely see the inflatables surrounding the speedboat.

Chris shut the loud engines off and Ray shortened the towing line of the tender to bring it closer to the speedboat. The outboards on the inflatables now surrounding the speedboat barely made a gurgling sound.

"Hi Chris! Ray! Good to see you guys" said the familiar voice behind the black balaclava.

"I guess you have us at a disadvantage behind that rag Rick" said Chris with some sarcasm.

"Well, you know how it is. The boys and I like to have a life outside work" responded Rick.

"Okay guys, one per boat and put a flotation device on them just in case they go overboard" Rick directed to the men on the black inflatables.

One by one they transferred Wilfredo, Jairo and Rodrigo in a very systematic order. First, they placed automatic flotation devices on them, then they checked the cable ties on their wrists and finally searched them for any hidden toys. They collected their phones and placed them in Ziplock bags. It wasn't until they were finished with each one before they transferred one to each boat and sat them in a centered seat.

Rick came onboard once the prisoners were secured on the boats to speak with Chris and Ray. He went to explain how they had been after these guys for some time and who they really were after was their boss.

Chris asked Rick if he had heard the name Machado. He mentioned how one of the prisoners had mentioned something about a witch of the mountain.

Rick told Chris and Ray that he was going to investigate the name and get clearance to brief them. He also went to explain about one of the prisoners being a midlevel smuggler out of Cartagena who already had some friends looking for him. Word was that they were also part of a human trafficking ring. They provided minors from Brazil, Colombia and Venezuela to buyers' market in the east.

"What's going to happen to these guys? will they be back out doing the same thing in a few months?" asked Ray.

"These guys are traveling on short leashes to our last class resort on the eastern coast of Cuba. There they will spend some time being debriefed and enjoying all the amenities the resort has to offer. Until they start singing" answered Rick with sarcasm written all over his face. "Then", he continued, "they will have their come to Jesus meetings with the law without extradition. They just wrote their own future."

"We have a present for you Rick" Chris said while showing Rick the stack of weapons and throwing the keys to the speedboat at him.

"Well, thank you! That is very kind of you, but I'm an open fisherman boat kind of guy myself. I'll tell you what. We'll add it to the pile of confiscated property we have been gathering form these bottom feeders" said Rick.

"Good!" said Chris, as he started to climb over the engine cover towards the tender.

"We may need your help in the near future with some non-biological findings that we don't want to fall into the hands of the corrupt government or armed forces here. Is that something you can help us with?" asked Ray to Rick.

Rick thought about it for a second and said: "Absolutely not! Buck Riley is your man for that. Tell him I said hi and that he still owes me. He'll help move your findings. After all, he's an expert in salvage, a bit on the gray way of doing things, but a good one."

Ray nodded and climbed on the tender with the towing line.

Rick started the engines and headed north towards the darkness where he came from.

"Where do you think they came from? Guantanamo is eight hundred miles from here. They don't have the range" asked Ray

I'm sure they have a cutter, A destroyer, an aircraft carrier or a submarine nearby providing them support. Chris replied and started the small outboard. "Let's pray we have enough juice on this tender to make it back to Picuda Grande."

The run back to Picuda Grande was uneventful. The moon had come out behind the islands and provided enough light to navigate in the night. A light northeast breeze made the run easier with the wind and spray from the waves behind them. A couple of times they heard dolphins or small whales coming up to the surface to exhale but could never see them.

"What do you want to do about those coins the girls found under the wreck?" Ray asked keeping a heading with the lights of the mainland.

"I'm not sure yet. Let's look tomorrow and see what else is there" replied Chris.

It was past midnight by the time they tied the tender to the old Chris Craft. Susana and Victoria looked over the railing when they heard the noise of the outboard.

"Good morning!" said Ray climbing up to the boat.

"And a very good morning to you too" replied Victoria. "What did you do with the speedboat and the passengers? Did you get rid of them?"

"That's not for us to determine. We only deliver. If this continues, we're going to have to start a franchise, RC Deliveries. How's that sound?" said Chris with a mysterious smile on his face.

"What have you ladies been up to this fine evening?" asked Ray.

"We have been cleaning the coins some more. Now we can see more engravings on them" answered Susana with excitement in her voice as she walked towards the table they had been working at.

"Are the captain and Eduardo sleeping?" asked Chris, almost whispering.

"Yes, they were out here with us for another hour and then they went to sleep once all the tanks were filled" answered Victoria.

They all walked over to the table to examine the coins.

"Definitely Spanish Doubloons!" said Ray as he turned around and was hypnotized by the hammock. "Good night you all."

Chris and the girls stayed up a bit longer looking at the details on the coins and trying to decipher some of the letters and shields on them. Fatigue started to sink in after a long night and it wasn't long before they all went to sleep.

PICUDA CHICA

CHAPTER 21

The laughing sea hags kept coming towards him in the barely lit cave as he woke up and the sun was coming out over Las Islas Caracas to the east. Coffee was brewing somewhere. He could smell it in the air. "Why the nightmares?" he thought to himself and quickly shook it off when he looked over the calm waters of the national park. The frigates were already up in the air chasing schools of fish from above. A small pod of dolphins swam by chasing mullets and a spotted sea ray jumped a good six feet out of the calm water. It was going to be another day at the office. There is no other place he'd rather be than out at sea. The morning ferry heading towards the island of Margarita went by with a gang of seagulls chasing it for free meals.

Chris started questioning some of the events from the previous night. What did Rick know about that Machado subject he was not saying? Why would Rick not offer to help them? Why were they taking the prisoners to Guantanamo? So many questions and no straight answers.

"Good morning sunshine!" Victoria said shading the sun and holding a glass of orange juice in front of him.

"Not yet, but I'm sure it will be" he said taking the glass of orange juice from her and walking to the stern of the boat to stretch.

Ray had gone for a swim early and was returning to the swimming platform. Chris stepped down and sat with his feet in the water.

"Are we off towards Little Picuda for a wreck dive this fine morning?" asked Ray, still breathing hard.

"Sure!" was all Morning Chris replied.

They ate more Cazon empanadas and fruits for breakfast along with conversations about the coins, treasures and the wreck dive.

"I can't get over how good these Cazon empanadas taste," said Chris. "It doesn't taste like shark at all. I don't know if it's the condiments they use to cook the stew or what, but it's delicious."

"What are the chances of one shipwreck sinking on top of the other?" asked Victoria.

"Let's not get very excited and carried away with that find," Ray said. "It may lead to nothing more than a few old gold coins. We would need a record of a sunken or missing ship in the area, or a finding that identifies provenance of the sunken ship. Without that, we're just punching in the dark. I don't believe those gold coins were inside or part of the cement shipwreck. There is a very slight chance that these coins came from under that wreck. There may be something else below it." Chris stopped for a second to look around for Eduardo and said:

"Eduardo, I saw you had an air nozzle attached to a high-pressure hose of the first stage of a regulator. You were using it to blow the inside of the first stage of a regulator. Do you think we can borrow it?"

"Yes! Sure, let me find it," answered Eduardo and went to the upper deck near the air compressor.

Eduardo stepped back down to the main deck and said: "Here, but you'll need to carry an extra tank with you. This rig will empty your tank in a few minutes, and faster under pressure."

"Thank you, Eduardo! We'll take an additional tank with us" said Ray. "Can you drop us at the site and catch us when we surface?"

"No problem!" said Eduardo.

"Okay, then! Now that we have a plan, let's get ready for a short run to Picuda Chica. We'll drop the anchor there and you can go and dive the wreck with the tender" suggested Captain Giovanni.

Everybody scrambled to help tidy up after breakfast and to make sure everything was secure on the deck. The girls went to change below when the engines started. After a few minutes, Captain Giovanni signaled Eduardo to bring the anchor chain up. There was rattling until the anchor was up and the captain reversed the props to back out of the cove. Once clear of the rocks, he throttled slowly forward southwest heading towards Picuda Chica.

Chris checked his phone for messages and missed calls and noticed he had three missed calls already this morning. One from Rick, another from General Pineda and another number he didn't recognize.

He listened to the messages: Rick wanted him to call him back and the general had left a message that was difficult to hear; something about fishing last night and to call him back.

He pressed the call button for Rick first.

"Is this secured?" asked Rick when he answered the call.

"It's encrypted Rick" answered Chris.

"Good! I wanted to thank you for the gifts from last night, and the ones that keep coming. They are starting to sing like Lola. One of those birds told us about a container arriving at the port of Tampa Bay today with one ton of pure coke hidden in rice bags" said Rick. "Which reminds me to warn you that you need to start watching your back. You stirred the witch's world with your gift to us."

"That's great Rick! Now, are you going to tell me more about this witch and who Machado is, or do I have to keep guessing?" asked Chris.

"It would be more fun to keep you guessing since it will become more dangerous as you start probing and asking questions, but I have something for you. Now, I don't want you to go around saying that I don't like to share."

"Rick! Enough with keeping me guessing. Start talking!" said Chris frustrated with Rick's games.

"Okay! Okay! Keep your panties on partner," said Rick with a laugh and continued,

"I had to run this by my superiors before bringing you up to date, that's why I couldn't tell you last night. There has been a lot of time and resources invested in this investigation and in trying to bring this cartel down.

"Cecilia Machado and The Witch of The Mountain are the same person. The boys you brought in last night were under her employment, just her puppets. She is the one behind the drug smuggling and the human trafficking ring. It's been hard on our teams because she keeps moving from one location to another. When she finds out a location is compromised, she moves on to the next one at random. She only uses burner phones, and she has ears everywhere, Cartagena, Cali, Medellin, San Andres, Panama, Miami and even Caracas and New York City. She believes that you owe her two boats, over a thousand kilos of cocaine, an old Land Cruiser, a bunch of guns and three of her grunts plus damages and interests. This is why I'm telling you that you need to be careful. The minute she finds out about the container you and Ray are dead men walking.

"Our analysts believe that she has been at her Cali location for the last three days based on some activities and movement of her informants and vehicles."

"Great!" Chris said.

"Have you contacted Buck?" Rick asked.

"Not yet, you were going to send me his phone number. Why do you ask?"

"That's right. I'll do it right now. I believe you should have Buck as your emergency exit strategy in case things get uglier around here" Rick said and continued to ask Chris, "Where and how did you get all those toys you were playing with last night? Wait, don't tell me. The less I know about that the better."

"Goodbye Rick. Thanks for all the great news" replied Chris.

"We're here to serve and entertain." said Rick with sarcasm.

Chris ended the call and called the general's number.

"Good morning general" Chris spoke into the phone when the general answered.

"Are you recovered from your party last night?" the general asked.

"Word travels fast around her too, general. Before I forget, thank you again for the package. It came in handy" Chris said.

"No worries, anything for an old friend of the family. Just be careful, you have shaken a tree so to speak. "Let me know if you need anything else."

"Thank you, general" Chris said. "How are the girls?"

Everyone is doing fine, doing their things, going on with life. You know how it is."

They said their goodbyes and finished the call.

It wasn't long by the time they were dropping the anchor along the southwest side of the island. They put on their wetsuits, loaded their gear on the tender and were on their way to the wreck site. While Eduardo steered the tender everyone else was putting their gear on and checking straps, hoses, inflators and deflators. Mask and fins went on last as Eduardo approached the wreck site. He saw the bottom change dramatically and on the screen of the fish finder and said: We're on top of the wreck.

All four divers rolled back in the water and dove except Chris who swam back to the tender and Eduardo handed him the additional eighty cubic feet tank with a hose hanging from the top. Eduardo had added a single strap to the side of the tank making it easier to carry under one arm.

By the time Chris was halfway down in the water column, Susana, Victoria and Ray were already on the bottom swimming towards the bow and the crevice where Susana had found the coins the day before. They were all looking around and gently moving away sand to the sides. Chris saw that the sand particles they were moving sank forward towards the bow of the shipwreck. That built a plan of attack in his mind.

When Chris descended to the bottom, he took all the air out of his vest, laid down on his stomach and opened the valve of the spare tank. Using his index finger on the trigger of the nozzle, he slowly applied pressure until air started to come out of it. He didn't want to let too much air out of the nozzle. He kept telling himself: "Slow is good! Like my friend Jesse in the content Keys says all the time".

When the sand he started to move forward of the shipwreck started to rise, the others caught up with that part of the plan and swam to his side or behind him. Nobody wanted to get sandblasted underwater. In a matter of minutes, the hole had doubled in size and now a full arm would fit. Chris pressed on but carefully observing what was being thrown up out of the hole. He started a sequence of letting the sand settle, inspect and continue spraying the sand with the air nozzle. Ray came closer, tapped on Chris shoulder and took over for a few more minutes. Chris kept an eye on the flowing sand.

More black rocks in different shapes started to appear buried in the sand. Ray stopped the airflow from the nozzle and stretched his arm inside the hole. He then handed the black rocks to Susana who already had her mesh bag open.

There was an elongated black rock he couldn't pull out, so he pointed at it with the air nozzle and blew more air around it. After a few seconds he stopped and looked again. The elongated shape seemed longer now. He tried to pull it out by wiggling slightly but it would not come out. Something was holding the end. He applied more air pressure.

After several attempts, the elongated rock gave, and he was able to pull it out of the sand. He guessed it measured just under two feet long and had a larger rock attached to it. When he pulled the final piece and held it up for inspection, it bent in different places. He turned and placed it in the mesh bag that Susan held open.

A few minutes later, Chris tapped Ray on the shoulder. Ray stopped blowing air at the sand and saw Chris extending his hand. Ray handed the hose with the nozzle and the spare tank to Chris who took over and continued blowing sand forward of the wreck.

Victoria assumed the position of the watch. She hung suspended by the buoyancy in her vest, and with her arms and legs crossed. When the light current took her too far, she would swim back closer and resume her position. She let the current turn her around slowly so that she could watch the surroundings. The visibility was about sixty to seventy feet, and she was able to observe the reef fish darting in and out of the wreck with curiosity as to what was going on. A couple of small reef sharks hung out in the background swimming back and forth on the other side of the shipwreck. A school of blue runners went darting over the wreck like they were being chased. It was a usual day on the reef.

Chris kept moving sand out of the way for another ten minutes. At this point he could fit half of himself in the hole they had dug. He stopped blowing the sand out after a few minutes and let everything settle. He handed the spare tank to Ray and maneuvered his head and shoulders into the hole. Now the faceplate of his mask was only inches from the bottom, but he was able to move his arms and shoulders inside the hole. He moved his hands back and forth near the bottom and more sand went to the sides. Once the sand settled, he could see what looked like the top of a drainage, dark and rusty in color. He kept moving the sand along the edges of it until he was able to see the whole rectangular piece. The openings between bars were about two inches. He could slide his fingers through them but not his whole hand. He pushed and slowly backed out of the hole. The first thing he did was to look at the pressure gauge of his instrument console and then at the computer on his wrist. Then he signaled, pointing two fingers towards his eyes and then pointing one finger towards the hole. Ray caught on and stuck his head inside the hole. A minute later Susana followed by Victoria peeked. It took Victoria an extra two minutes to back out of the hole, and when she lifted her head, she handed more rocks to Susana who placed them inside the mesh bag.

Ray pointed at the computer on his wrist and signaled it was time to ascend towards the surface. They were close to reaching the non-decompression limit for a diver at that depth. As a group, they slowly ascended and slowed down as they got closer to the surface. The outboard of the tender could be heard at a distance and they started to look up before breaking the surface. One by one they handed Eduardo their SCUBA rigs and climbed into the tender by kicking their fins, laying on their stomachs on the pontoons and then sitting. They all laughed and told short tales or comments about the dive on the way back to the boat. Every one of them with the same type of question in mind: What else is down there? Where did it come from? How old is it?

It was past noon by the time they were back on board. Captain Giovanni had prepared ham and cheese sandwiches and fruit plates for lunch. They ate and continued their tales about the dive and the artifacts which Susana and Victoria had placed immediately in a tray to start the cleaning process.

"That cement ship must have gone down on top of an old shipwreck that was probably already buried in the sand. It could have crashed some of the upper structure of the old shipwreck. That drain plate must have been on one of its decks and when the cement ship came crashing down, the deck where the drain plate was must have been squeezed onto the next lower deck. We're probably looking at the stern area of the old shipwreck. That's my theory" said Ray. "I guess the question is: what do we want to do next?"

"How are we doing on the data uploads? Are we all caught up?" Chris asked.

"We are caught up on the invasive species project up to our last dive yesterday. All the specimen photos are loaded up too" responded Victoria.

"Except for this last morning dive, all the others have been uploaded to the Swedish servers." replied Ray.

Chris thought about the whole scenario for a minute and said: "Let's make one more dive and clear more sand around that hole. We'll split up so that we can cover a larger area."

Chris was about to say that if they only had another nozzle, when Eduardo walked up to him and said: "I don't have another one of those nozzles, but I rigged this one that you can also use." He handed Chris another hose with a different type of nozzle. This one, you had to bend it sideways for the air to blow out of the hose. It didn't have a visible trigger, but it would work just the same.

"If the current continues running in the same direction, you and Susana can blow out one corner and Victoria and I will work on the other corner" Ray continued. "We just must try and not be in each other's way. Also, let's also bring another mesh bag and a couple of prybars.

"This might be a bigger job than what we can handle with what we have on board. It may require heavy salvaging equipment" Chris said. "One more dive and we'll go from there. Planning, we need to start thinking about moving these artifacts and where we want them to end up."

"I don't believe handing this find over to the government is a good idea these days with all the corruption and vandalism. We need to think about the next logical place" said Giovanni.

"What do you guys think about the Museo Naval del Caribe in Cartagena, Colombia"? Chris asked. "We can arrange to be flown out of here and into Cartagena. We must first all agree that this is the right thing to do at this time. I'm not trying to lead anyone, but that museum has the most historical records and artifacts around here. I know someone there who can help us with the research."

"Look at this!" Susana said with excitement looking inside of the trays.

Everyone gathered around the wet table to see. Sections of the elongated rocks were starting to dissolve exposing a gold chain almost an inch thick. Hanging from one of the links of the chain was what started to look like a brooch or a medal.

"How much time do you need to get ready for the next dive?" Ray asked Susana.

"Another ten minutes and I can place this on the wash tray" answered Susana.

"Okay! Fifteen minutes and we'll start loading the gear in the tender. Will that work Eduardo?" Ray asked.

"No problem! I'll start loading the tanks."

Chris went up on the bridge with his phone and found the number for Buck Reilly that Rick had sent him and punched it.

"Last Resort! How may I help you?" The voice of a woman answering the call said.

"Buck Reilly, please" said Chris

"Hold please" replied the woman and then shouted at someone at a distance: "Reilly! It's for you."

A couple of minutes later, Buck Reilly spoke: "Buck!"

"Buck, my name is Chris Dunn. Rick suggested I give you a call," explained Chris over the phone.

"You're in trouble and need help, right? Call 911." Buck said.

"No, wait, let me explain some more please," Chris spoke urgently.

"You have two minutes. I am a busy man."

"We found some things underwater that are very old in a place where it wouldn't be wise to bring in the authorities in on it. We need help with transportation" explained Chris.

"Okay, okay, I'll give you two more minutes of my time since you got my attention. This is sounding more and more like an extraction from a communist country" said Buck, now a bit more interested.

"Well, yes, sort of. We are inside the National Park of Mochima in Venezuela. We are scientific divers working on several projects. While doing some field work down here, we ran into what we think is an undocumented shipwreck holding some old valuables. We have just started to bring some of them to the surface and have agreed to turn it over to the Museo Naval del Caribe in Cartagena.

"Who are we? And how much cargo are we talking about?" asked Buck

"It will be four of us with our dive gear and it's hard to say right now about the findings. I believe it will be a sample of not more than 10 or 12 coins and some jewelry. It's Just a sample to research dates and provenance of the findings" Chris went to explain.

"When?" asked Buck.

"Tomorrow if possible" answered Chris.

"So, you want me to stop what I'm doing right now, jump on a plane, fly over thirteen hundred miles, avoid detection flying into Venezuelan waters, pick you and your buddies up and fly you six hundred and sixty miles to Cartagena with contraband. You must really have the wrong number. You need to call one eight hundred God Save Me" explained Buck with sarcasm.

"Well, now that you put it that way, yes. I am only following up on a suggestion from your friend Rick. He said you were very resourceful in situations like these. Thank you for your time and for listening."

A few seconds of silence passed and Buck came back. "Okay, okay! I'll call you tomorrow with a number where you can send coordinates to for the pickup. I need calm waters and at least a mile for landing and takeoff. If we get shot, you pay for the plane. Understood?

"Yes! exclaimed Chris."

"Oh, and one more thing: Rick is not my friend. He is a pain in my neck."

Thank you, Buck! You will not regret it."

"Somehow, I've heard that many times when I did regret it" said Buck and he hung up.

Chris, not wanting to get all their hopes up, kept the outcome of the phone call to himself instead of sharing it with the others. By the time he came down from the bridge,

Ray, Susana and Victoria were starting to get into their wetsuits. He joined them in a happy mood with somewhat of a plan evolving inside his head.

They loaded the rest of their gear and headed to the wreck site. It was midafternoon by the time they were on top of the wreck, and they were starting to sweat inside their wetsuits. Once they entered the water, the relief of the cool water entering their wetsuits made them feel more comfortable. They dove straight down to the bow of the cement shipwreck, laid the additional tanks on the sand and started blowing sand out of the hole they had made on the previous dive. They took turns with the air nozzles and slowly made progress by blowing sand away from the hole.

After ten minutes into the dive, they stopped the flow of air into the sand and waited a couple of minutes for the particles to settle. Chris and Ray took the prybars and inserted them on each side of the metal drain. As they put some pressure on the bars, the drain plate crumbled like it was made of Styrofoam for a movie stunt. They slowly removed the pieces out of the way and outside of the hole, which at this point a large person could sit inside of it.

Ray slowly crawled inside the hole that the drain was blocking. He was able to fit his head inside for a look. A second later he was signaling with one hand for a mesh bag. He pulled the bag in front of him and started filling it. When he slowly backed out of the hole, Chris went next with the other mesh bag.

With both bags half-filled and only ten minutes of bottom time left on their dive computers, they started swimming towards the surface. Susana and Victoria brought the spare tanks with the air hoses and Chris and Ray struggled bringing the mesh bags to the surface. They had to add more air to their buoyancy compensator vest to make some progress on the swim to the surface. The danger of losing any of the weight inside the bags would have sent them to the surface at a much faster pace than they needed to. Instead of having the heavy mesh bags hanging from their hands, they hugged them like a very old bottle of aged rum.

Eduardo was already helping Susana and Victoria climb inside the tender by the time they surfaced. Carefully, they handed the bags up to them by pushing them from the bottom. They rested still in the water for a few minutes before getting out onto the tender.

With a heavy breath, Ray said: "I'm sure there's a lot more, but I believe this is all we need for now to prove its date and provenance. We'll come back with the right equipment and salvage it."

The rest just nodded and started peeling the tops of their wetsuits on the ride back to the boat.

Back on the boat they unloaded the tender and rinsed their gear. When Susana went to lift one of the mesh bags with the findings, the bottom of the bag opened and spread its contents on the deck. Chris and Susana started picking up the pieces and Ray and Victoria went inside the galley.

Susana started placing some of the pieces inside the first container with the acidic solution while Chris carefully lifted the other bag and placed it on the table. Captain Giovanni and Eduardo were already gathering around the table by the time Ray and Victoria came out with drinks, cheese and crackers.

"Salud!" Victoria said, raising her glass and the others followed.

"Excelente!" Chris said after taking a sip of his drink.

They all stood around savoring the moment in the early evening surrounded by the beauty of the islands, the sunset and the water around them. Eduardo started moving empty tanks away for refills and the captain went to start the generator and cook dinner.

"Have you ever been to Cartagena?" Chris asked Susana and Victoria knowing that Ray had been there on several occasions.

"No!" I hear it's nice," said Susana focused on the cleaning process of the pieces.

"No, never had" answered Victoria.

"Is that a place that you would like to visit anytime in the near future?" asked Chris.

They both nodded suspecting what was coming.

"How about tomorrow? We'll fly out of here and fly into Cartagena tomorrow with the findings and do the research on these artifacts" Chris explained.

"And you have a magic carpet, right?" inquired Victoria with a smile.

"Well, you could call it that for now" answered Chris. "I made a call earlier, before we went on our dive. It was suggested that I call this guy named Buck in Key West and ask him to fly us four, our gear and the artifacts out of here and into Cartagena. Is that something you would like to do? I am about to say something very selfish here. I'd rather get you out of here than worry about some version of those goons coming back for you. But it's your decision to be made."

"How much time do I have to pack my stuff?" asked Victoria excited.

Susana was still focused on the cleaning process of the artifacts. She stood upright and said: "I'm not leaving this stuff out of my sight. Look!"

She had managed to clean three small bars of melted gold and five of silver, along with more gold chains and over thirty-five gold coins. Some still had accumulated sediment over them but were in the process of dissolving and falling off. They all stare at the artifacts for a few minutes and Ray said: "Cartagena, here we come."

Chris went to check messages on his phone and noticed a missed call from another unknown number. Thinking it might have been Buck asking for coordinates, he redialed the number.

After a couple of rings, a voice at the other end of the call said: "I am coming after you Chris Dunn and after your buddy Ray too. I don't easily forget, and you owe me. I am coming to collect from you and your friends. You will pay for the rest of your life. I will make an example of you. I have a reputation to maintain. You can run all you want from me, but I will find you." The call ended.

Chris knew that one was not one of his recent dreams. That sounded real. He started thinking about the mess he had gotten himself and his friend into when the phone in his hand started ringing.

Expecting the same voice, he answered: "Hello!"

"Chris? Buck here. Text me the coordinates to this number. I'll be there by late afternoon if I don't run into any hiccups."

"I will text you the numbers Buck! Thank you again."

"Don't thank me just yet. We're just getting started." replied Buck before he finished the call.

Chris felt relief. He texted Buck the latitude and Longitude for Ensenada La Cienaga on the southern side of the island of Chimana Grande. He then went to mix another rum and coke round for the crew and give them the good news.

"We are flying out of here tomorrow afternoon if all goes according to plan folks. So, start getting your gear and bags ready. Let's find a way to pack all this stuff in a conspicuous way so it doesn't attract attention. It seems our new friend Buck Reilly came through."

They all tossed and said: "Cartagena!"

"Wow! What kind of rum is this, again?" asked Chris with a smile.

"Excelente!" shouted Ray, Susana and Victoria in unison and they all laughed.

While enjoying their drinks, they all started rounding up their gear and packing it in their dive bags.

The scent of garlic, parsley and basil was in the air as captain Giovanni came out of the galley with a large tray steaming and said: Fettuccine al Pomodoro for tonight with garlic bread and Caesar salad. Come and get it.

They had all spent a lot of energy on their dives. They didn't feel like recreational or observational dives anymore. It had been more like underwater work dives. After relaxing for a bit and running around getting light chores completed, they ate like a battalion. They all went for second servings.

After dinner, the girls started to plan the trip with phone calls to family and with colleagues asking to cover work for them.

Chris and Ray sat in the hammocks and Chris said:" I got a nasty call from Machado. She wants to dance. She' s starting to chase us soon. We must watch our backs."

"Oh. Oh!" Said Ray.

"I am beginning to debate about Cartagena being a good idea" said Chris.

"We won't know until we are there playing around the walls of the old city" answered Ray.

They both sat there in silence for another ten minutes and Ray was out.

Chris got out of his hammock and went to find captain Giovanni on the bridge. He was looking at weather forecasts and long-range radar scans.

"What are we thinking?" asked Giovanni when Chris stepped onto the bridge.

"We'd like you to keep a low profile and tell anyone who asks about us that we drove back to Caracas. None of us feel comfortable right now turning these artifacts into government agencies and much less the military. We want to find a good place for the artifacts where we can research provenance and dating before we turn it over to a good historical records organization."

"We decided that the Museo Naval del Caribe in Cartagena would be as good a place as any nearby. We are having a friend picking us up tomorrow at Ensenada La Cienaga on the southern side of the island of Chimana Grande. He's flying in on a G-21 Goose. After he hits the water, we can have Eduardo take us in the tender with our gear, bags and artifacts to the plane. He will then fly us to Cartagena. We want to come back with help and complete the salvage with you and all the formalities needed. Would you be okay with that plan? Any thoughts?"

The captain thought for a minute in silence and nodding his head he said: "I believe that's a good plan Chris. Just don't forget about us. I trust you more than those corrupt thieves calling themselves the government. What do you need from me tomorrow?"

"If you can get us to Chimana Grande in the morning, it would be great" Chris replied. He got up from the bench seat and before he left, he asked the captain: "If you can think of a good plan to conceal those artifacts down there for travel, let me know. I don't want to create an international conflict just yet."

"Very good! If I can think of something, I'll let you know" said Giovanni

"Good night captain and thank you for everything. If I ever get into the food and beverage business, you will be my first choice of chef."

CHAPTER 22

Cecilia Machado was hysterically shouting at everyone and barking right and left.

"Those gringos don't know who they are messing with. I'll show them a good time if that's what they're looking for." She spoke to herself as she paced up and down the balcony of one of her hideouts in the mountains. She had tried several times to call and speak with Rodrigo, but he never answered his phone. Then he asked one of his grunts to find Jairo's phone number for her. She tried Jairo's phone several times and all the calls went straight to voice messages. Her level of frustration kept rising.

Cursing about giving up on her employees and that they were good for nothing, she opened another burner phone and activated it. She then placed a call to one of her government officials on her payroll in Venezuela. A director of police intelligence.

"Señora Machado, so glad to hear your voice."

"How did you know it was me calling Miguel?" asked the frustrated Cecilia.

"There is a reason I am the director of police intelligence services Cecila. I'm not just another pretty face in Caracas."

"Miguel, I need the phone number of someone making calls out of the islands of Parque Nacional Mochima to outside of the country in the last three or four days. Most likely from the western islands and the region of Santa Fe. Search the logs on those towers or whatever it is you do" she demanded.

"Have you misplaced your phone again Cecilia?" asked Miguel with a sarcastic laugh.

"Don't toy with me Miguel. I am not in the mood today. Can you do this or not?"

"Let me see what I can find out Cecilia. I'll call you back in a couple of hours. Is this a good number to call you back?" asked director Miguel.

I will call you in two hours Miguel."

"Mierda!" Cecilia said and made a kicking motion into the air with her right foot, one of her sandals went out flying over the balcony to the patio below and she shouted: "Muertos! Estan Muertos." She took the other sandal off her left foot and threw it out over the balcony.

Two hours later, after a good soak in the jacuzzi pool and a shower, Cecilia called the director of police intelligence back with a new burner phone.

"Miguelito, you better have some good news for me. I don't feel like reorganizing today."

"Yes Cecilia, as a matter of fact, I do" responded Miguel. "There's only one strange out of the country number with several calls in the last few days, short calls too."

Miguel gave her the number of the phone and Cecilia ended the call. Immediately she punched in the number. There was no answer at the other end and the call went to voice messages.

Cecilia started to get irritated again and shouted at her assistant: "We're moving Bernardo, get things ready. Call the pilots too. Have them get the plane ready. We're going after those gringos and get some guns too, lots of guns." She turned around to go into her closet to get dressed, but stopped and asked her assistant Bernardo: "Where is the container? Is it still moving? Don't you dare take your eyes off that tracking. You let me know the second it stops."

"The container just arrived in the Port of Tampa Bay a couple of minutes ago, Señora Machado" Bernardo said while looking down.

"Imbecil! Now you tell me?" she shouted at Bernardo. "I want to know the second it starts moving by truck. No more excuses."

Pacheco, Cecilia's driver, was standing by the door when she and Bernardo walked out to the circular driveway of the ranch house. "What are you waiting for?" she shouted at the driver. "Vamos! Camine!" She climbed into the white Mercedes Benz G Class SUV with bulletproof glass windows. A second black SUV was parked behind and four men were loading up bags and followed Cecilias car.

At a private landing strip outside of a town called Medialuna, sixty miles east of Cartagena, a Cessna Citation Longitude was waiting with a crew reading the plane for takeoff. The two Mercedes SUVs pulled up a few feet from the jet and Cecilia and her entourage boarded. Cecilia was offered a glass of Champagne that she turned down and mumbled: "We're not celebrating! Not yet!".

"We are ready for takeoff, Señora Cecilia. Where would you like to go today?" asked the pilot standing straight by the door of the cockpit.

"To Puerto La Cruz" answered Cecilia"

The pilot turned around, closed the door to the cockpit and started his takeoff process. "Puerto La Cruz, Barcelona – BLA" he instructed his copilot.

During takeoff Cecilia opened another burner and punched the number that director Miguel had given her. This time there was an answer after three rings.

"I am coming after you Chris Dunn and after your buddy Ray too. I don't easily forget, and you owe me. I am coming to collect from you and your friends. You will pay for the rest of your life. I will make an example of you. I have a reputation to maintain. You can run all you want from me, but I will find you." She then ended the call.

After takeoff, Bernardo got off his seat and stood beside Cecilia's seat. He waited until she finished her calls to inform her: "Señora Cecilia, the container was confiscated by the DEA in the Port of Tampa. It seems they were tipped off according to my contacts. I don't know what happened."

Cecilia threw the phone at Bernardo, hitting him on the forehead. Bernardo sat back in his seat and closed his eyes. He knew how much mayhem was about to explode.

CHAPTER 23

"Good morning sunshine! Victoria said to Chris. He was in the process of waking up after a shower and putting on clean shorts and a shirt before walking back out on the deck. Victoria handed him a glass of orange juice and walked back to the galley.

"Thank you! Victoria for spoiling me" Chris replied.

Captain Giovanni started the engines of the old Chris Craft and let them warm up for a few minutes.

Ray and Eduardo were engaged in a conversation about tanks and tank valves. Eduardo was removing an air valve off the top of an air tank while Ray held the tank with his hands around it.

"What do you think Chris?" asked Ray.

"About what?" answered Chris.

"About emptying a couple of SCUBA tanks, removing the tank valves and placing the artifacts inside the empty tanks?" asked Ray.

"That is a very clever idea, Ray" answered Chris. "That's one of the reasons I like about hanging out with you. I get smarter."

"So, it's not just for the looks that I have?" asked Ray laughing and getting back to the task at hand.

"How about weight? How heavy will all that make the tanks?" Chris asked.

"We are about to find out" Ray replied.

Susana and Victoria were packing their gear and had their bags with clothing and computers on the deck ready to be loaded into the tender.

Chris and Ray, with the help of Eduardo inserted most of the artifacts inside the two tanks and sealed them with their valves. A few items didn't fit through the neck of the tanks.

Ray lifted each tank gauging their weights and said: "Not too bad. A bit heavier than a full tank, but you would have to have one full of air to compare and tell the difference."

"Okay Eduardo let's weigh anchor and get out of here. It will be a short trip to Chimana Grande." Shouted captain Giovanni from above. Eduardo moved to the bow and engaged the windlass to lift the anchor from the sandy bottom. As soon as the anchor was secured Giovanni turned the boat around and headed east towards Chimana Grande. With only six miles to navigate, they were there in under half an hour.

Giovanni steered the boat to the other side of Playa Puinare, but not too far from the island so as not to block the entrance to the Ensenada La Cienaga. He wanted to leave the hydroplane enough room to maneuver.

A midsize jet plane flew over them at a low altitude, turned and came back towards the boat. They were all looking up and could almost see the faces of the people inside the plane. The plane banked right as they flew over Giovani's boat and continued inland towards Lecherias.

"That was kind of close, Friends of yours?" asked Susana.

"A bit too close for me too. No, I don't have friends with corporate jets" Chris said, thinking about the threatening call he had from Cecilia Machado earlier.

An hour later Chris' phone rang, and he pulled it out of a pocket of his cargo shorts and answered: "Buck?"

"I am on approach. You can't see me yet since I'm flying very low over La Tortuga Island. I should be hitting the water in about twenty minutes. You won't see me coming until I turn onto the island. Are you guys ready to board? Asked Buck over the phone with the background noise of the plane engines.

"We'll be standing by Buck" answered Chris and the call ended.

"It sounds like our ride is here" said Ray.

We are on in twenty. That was Buck." Chris said to the group.

They started loading the tender with Eduardo's help and saying their goodbyes to captain Giovanni. Chris handed the captain a small nylon bag with the coins that didn't fit through the valve holes of the air tanks and said: "Keep this quiet captain and thank you again for everything."

As they were boarding the tender Buck Reilly's G-21 Goose flew over the boat and he banked left and right, turned around and flew straight towards the cove of Ensenada La Cienaga.

"What a beautiful view" Chris thought, admiring the lines and the impressive old airplane landing on the water. "Our magic carpet is here" he shouted and boarded the tender.

Eduardo steered the tender at a slow speed because of all the extra weight and did not want to get his passengers wet with the spray of the waves. By the time he got closer to the amphibious flying boat, Buck had already turned the 16-foot boat plane around and was pointing out of the cove.

Ray held the tender against the plane while the others started handing gear to Buck who was standing by the open door of the plane. Buck was wearing a Hawaiian shirt, khaki shorts, no shoes and a red cap with the Last Resort logo on it. His long hair hanging behind the red cap.

Once all the bags were inside the plane, Susana, Victoria and Chris boarded from the tender. Buck instructed the girls to store the bags behind the last row of seats and secured them with the nets hanging across.

Ray asked Eduardo to hold the tender close to the plane while he handed the first SCUBA tank to Chris.

"Woo! Woo! That's a no, no! Those tanks are not going inside this plane unless they are very empty" shouted Buck over the noise of the engines.

Chris and Ray looked at each other and smiled. Ray handed the second tank to Chris who turned around and said to Buck: "They are empty, but then again not" and he gave Buck a mischievous smile. Buck got the message and they both laughed.

Ray took three bills from his shorts' pocket, handed them to Eduardo and said: "Thank you for all you help Eduardo. We'll see you soon." He boarded the plane and pushed the tender away from the door.

"Welcome to The Beast. Find a seat, secure yourselves with the seatbelts and pray that we are not overloaded" said Buck to the group before he turned towards the pilot seat. "Chris, you are flying copilot today."

"Why does he call it The Beast?" asked Victoria to Susana. "I have no idea," answered Susana lifting her shoulders and her eyebrows.

Everyone got settled and fastened their seatbelts. Buck revved the engines up slowly and they started moving over the water faster and faster. He also instructed Chris to wear a headset hanging behind the copilot seat. Chris placed the headset over his head and adjusted the speakers over his ears and the microphone closer to his mouth. "Can you hear me?" Buck spoke into the microphone. Chris gave him a thumbs up and said: "Loud and clear".

When Buck was water-landing The Beast south of Chimana Grande, Cecilia Machado and four of his goons had boarded a fifty-foot Nor-Tech 500 Sport powered with five three hundred horse Mercury Racing outboards at Marina Imbuca in El Morro. They were rounding El Morro and were heading out to Chimana Grande when they saw the G-21 Goose lining up for a water landing.

Cecilia pointed at the beautiful plane and shouted over the noise of the engines: "Faster, faster you idiots. They are getting away"

"Are you expecting visitors?" Buck asked Chris over the headsets.

"Well, maybe yes, maybe no. It's a fifty-fifty thing right now. Why?" asked Chris.

"How upset are those guys at you? Did you forget to pay your hotel bill?" said Buck pointing at the silver and orange Nor-Tech 500 Sport coming at them.

Buck revved the engines up some more and the pontoons under the wings started to come off the water trailing a spray. A minute later The Beast was completely off the water on a collision course with the Nor-Tech 500 Sport coming at them. Buck pulled on the steering column and pushed on the right pedal and the plane gained altitude and banked to the right for a better look at the boat.

Chris saw what Cecilia Machado looked like for the first time. She was lifting a fist up and pointed it at them. A couple of her grunts reached for their guns, but by the time they tried to aim their guns, the G-21 Goose banked the other way gaining more altitude and flew away towards the east. They didn't stand a chance of hitting anything from a moving boat to a moving plane with their guns.

"I believe your fifty-fifty thing just changed to your advantage" came Buck over the headset.

"All thanks to you Buck, all thanks to you" Chris said and started to enjoy the ride. Flying low over the islands of the national park of Mochima, Chris could only guess as to why Christopher Colombus had named that country "The Small Venice". Venezuela. He imagined after weeks of being at sea crossing the Atlantic Ocean, encountering these beautiful islands and the northern coast of South America with their beautiful beaches, dramatic cliffs and green mountains in the background.

He also thought about what was waiting for them in Cartagena, Colombia. Although him and Ray had spent sometime there years ago, he could not imagine what to expect. Were they going to be able to find more information about the shipwreck below the cement ship? Will Cecilia Machado follow them with her revenge? Chris closed his eyes for a few seconds but none of the answers materialized. Buck kept the plane at a low altitude, and he just enjoyed the beauty of the scenery of Mochima knowing that his friends were safe from the monster. He didn't know for how long.

ABOUT THE AUTHOR

RICK CAMERON was born in Houston, Texas and lives in the Tampa Bay of Florida where many of the Chris Dunn and Ray Salas adventures started. When asking others what Rick does for fun when he is not writing, most would say that his response would be: "I like to play by the water, on the water or under the water." Rick is an avid fisherman, scuba diver and boater. One day Rick started writing about his travels, friends and adventures around many of the Caribbean islands and the coasts of North, Central and South America. He has not been able to stop.

Next
in this series...

Cartagena

WA

www.ingramcontent.com/pod-product-compliance
Lightning Source LLC
Chambersburg PA
CBHW071600110726
47908CB00007B/2177